CW00448956

A YEAR IN SUBURBIA

By the same author

The Secret Lemonade Drinker
I Have a Complaint to Make
The Sinner's Congregation
The Nudists
In the Midday Sun
The Tax Exile
A Village Called Sin
The Comedy Hotel
The Holiday
The Mystery of Men
The Power of Women
The Man Who Won

A YEAR IN SUBURBIA

Guy Bellamy

ROBERT HALE · LONDON

First published in Great Britain 2007

ISBN 978-0-7090-8496-9

Robert Hale Limited
Clerkenwell House
Clerkenwell Green
London EC1R 0HT

www.halebooks.com

2 4 6 8 10 9 7 5 3 1

Typeset in 11/16pt Palatino
Printed and bound in Great Britain by
Biddles Limited, King's Lynn

For Trevor Hunt

Muchas gracias

JANUARY

January is always unwelcome and
should be abolished.
– *Calvin Orsi*

Thursday 1 January

Edging with all available reluctance towards my fiftieth birthday I find that my view of the world is coloured by a profound and subversive conviction that the rewards are going to the wrong people. This may seem a somewhat jaundiced approach to the new year – quite contrary to the *joie de vivre* which the anniversary is supposed to generate – but the year has not started well.

Instead of waking up in bed this morning, a practice I have adhered to for years, I woke up on the sofa this afternoon and encountered some difficulty in getting up. When I eventually achieved a wobbly perpendicular and strolled across to the mirror to survey my ravaged countenance I saw a message Sellotaped to my forehead: GOOD-BYE. It said GOOD-BYE in the mirror! Emma had written it backwards so that I could read it as I studied my hungover reflection.

I removed the message and then found that standing up didn't suit me so returned to the sofa and sat down. If this was my wife walking out on me it seemed a particularly brusque way of doing it. I struggled to remember what events led up to her sudden disappearance. I have a rat-trap memory for the most tedious details from the past – election results, sporting triumphs, disasters, natural and man-made – but yesterday was beyond my reach.

Eventually, as I emerged from what had evidently been a

very deep sleep, I was able to work out that if today was 1 January, which for some reason was the only fact that my mind was clinging to, yesterday was probably New Year's Eve and somewhere among the celebrations there must have been a party.

It all came back to me then – at least, some of it did. Emma had inveigled me into appearing at the Westacotts' soirée. The Westacotts are her rich friends. Charles, a short, busy man with a Hitleresque moustache, was the sort of person who knows whether the dollar is weak or strong and what macroeconomics are and, if you are not pretty nimble, he will tell you about it. He is an MP and, like most MPs, shows a tremendous concern for the human race without actually liking anyone he meets. The Westacotts are a driven couple but with different objectives. Janet's idea of a busy day is a massage, a leg wax and a manicure, and she spends a lot of her time on her sunbed, blinded by two slices of cucumber. Last night she was wearing a sequined dress with crystal stilettos and diamond ear-rings, the whole ensemble costing about £5,000. God knows what little sidelines Charles had organized in the City to fund her absurd extravagance.

He came up to me quite early on like a man with seven watches up his sleeve, and announced that herons were nicking his koi carp. My simulated dismay at this airborne larceny seemed to satisfy him, and he moved on hurriedly as if my vote was in the bag. The funny thing about this bogus twerp is that he is a Labour MP with a poverty-stricken constituency in the north of England. There was no chance of the Westacotts living among his impoverished voters there.

Their ivy-covered mansion in which about thirty of us were marooned was exquisitely furnished, but all I could see last night in the light from some perfumed floating candles was alcohol – champagne in buckets, wine, sweet-scented bottles of gin, innocent-looking vodka, bacardi, bourbon and old reliable, the dark menace of Scotch, for which I misguidedly opted.

Janet appeared by my side as I was refilling my glass. The Westacotts were obviously working the room.

'How are you, Janet?' I asked. For a woman of forty she looked sensational – blonde, sun-tanned, radiant, youthful – but as she devoted most of her time to working on her appearance this was hardly surprising.

'I'm a lot better, Mark, since I discovered Reiki,' she said quietly, as if admitting to some secret vice. 'Reiki has given me the energy to seek contentment.'

I imagined that Reiki was a swarthy mid-European with a lazy eye and gigantic sexual equipment, but it turned out to be a type of massage. I endured the subsequent panegyric about its mysterious qualities, but soon it was time for my hostess to move on.

I looked round for my wife, but could only see her small fat friend Phoebe, a lady of uncertain sexuality, drinking miserably on her own in a corner. I went across.

'Have you seen Emma?' I asked.

'Emma?'

'You remember. The lady I married.'

She lowered the glass from her lips. 'Don't take the piss out of me, Mark, just because I'm drunk.'

I turned to get away, but she put a restraining hand on my arm. 'Don't go. I've got something to tell you. I'm writing a novel. You can sell it in your shop.'

'They have to be published before I can do that,' I told her.

'Oh, they'll publish it. They'll probably film it. It's a fascinating tale.'

'A Sapphic saga?' I suggested.

'Not at all. The heroine is a married woman. Or rather was.

The refuse collectors have just found her husband in the wheelie bin.'

'That sounds promising. Is he dead? Or is he trying to escape?'

'Oh, he's dead. She hasn't killed him; she's just trying to save on funeral expenses.'

'So she's put him out with the rubbish?'

'Appropriate, don't you think?' said this lachrymose dumpling with an evil grin.

'My wife might,' I had to admit. 'Have you seen her?'

I escaped as she shook her head and went over for another refill. I felt like a captured animal, but the Westacotts' parties, which were hard to get into, were also difficult to slip out of; there were too many watching eyes.

My wife's disappearance was assuming the proportions of a mystery I should investigate, but two things stopped me. I could hardly prowl round the Westacotts' private rooms – the party's perimeters were clear enough. And Emma would react badly if she thought I was checking up on her in some way. If she wanted my company she would know where to look.

I could hear my socially voracious hostess extolling the virtues of feng shui to a woman who looked like a model but was actually a rising star in the financial world. I went across past clinking glasses to where they were standing.

'Do you know where Emma is?' I asked.

Janet turned slowly and with perceptible reluctance. You weren't supposed to interrupt her.

'I believe she's in the conservatory with Rupert,' she said, and turned back to the pretty woman who knew about money.

It must have been at this moment that my memory deserted me because I don't remember a thing after that.

Sitting on the sofa and wondering who Rupert was, the lack

of recall worried me. Wasn't this the alarm bell that should jangle deafeningly in the head of a potential alcoholic?

Only one thing seemed clear: serving no useful purpose, I had been consigned to matrimonial oblivion. Oddly enough, I refused to be depressed by this. Given the stultifying routine which filled my days, my wife's abrupt defection became in my raddled mind a welcome diversion.

Memo to self: Get a life.

Friday 2 January

I'm going broke. I bought this bookshop with a bank loan twenty-five years ago in a determined rush to work for myself. The bank loan has been repaid, which is just as well because I'd never find the repayments in today's takings. Even as I study the plunging trajectory on my financial graph I'm not quite sure what went wrong. Of course, we live in a post-print age, and for those who can still read without moving their lips there are bigger and better bookshops which can find on their computers the most obscure tomes. I don't have a computer; I consult catalogues.

Today, bookshops like mine are places where people come in to get out of the rain, and feign an interest in Nabokov until the downpour stops; or where people who don't read buy books as presents for friends who don't read. Running one sometimes seems like throwing a party to which nobody comes.

The only certain income arrives from the comfortable flat upstairs where I have a tenant, Mrs Pringle, an overweight cheerful lady who reads books. Her rent is low because I can call on her at any time to run the shop if I am away.

It was only when I reached this disintegrating dream this morning that I made the connection between the financial crisis that looms and Emma's disappearance. I wasn't thinking too clearly yesterday. She had obviously vamoosed because she was tired of living in a world of diminishing returns, of self-denial and limited options. But how would flight improve her bank balance?

On the mat as I opened the shop door was a Christmas card from Australia – with snow on. Why would an Australian Christmas card feature snow? It was from an old school friend, Luke Dyson, who had quit Britain nearly thirty years ago, having fallen for a stockily built blonde from Brisbane who performed sexual acts on him that he had not encountered in our small market town. The air fare prevented my appearance at his wedding, but we had continued to correspond intermittently over the years.

I made my way through shelves of books, colourful in cover if not in content, to the back of the shop where I have a desk that is concealed from the customers by more books. I can sit here and do the paperwork (or crosswords), drink coffee, invent amusing verses, make phone calls, study catalogues or flip through the hopeful offering of the latest literary star.

It isn't, if you think about it, a very healthy existence, being deficient in the fresh air and exercise departments that are reputedly essential for strength, vigour and well-being. But I've given up on all that. Five years ago, after a lifetime of dependable good health, I began to receive some unwelcome reminders that my sojourn on this planet was not as open-ended as I had hoped. The reminders arrived as little parcels of sickness or physical inconvenience which without being serious were always enough to take the shine off a day or two, particularly as they occurred mysteriously in pairs. I made a list of them. January: toothache and influenza. February: lumbago and diarrhoea (an unfortunate concatenation, with one demanding swift movement and the other preventing it).

March: colic and chilblains. A sense of parts seizing up, fuel running out and wheels coming off began to preoccupy me as I ruefully contemplated a new and unexpected period of my life during which I would gradually slither into infirmity and decrepitude.

But April failed to deliver the expected double dose of misery and arrived instead with warm sunshine, waving daffodils and the promise that life had more to offer than a graceful decline towards senescence. I grabbed the reprieve. I was only forty-five. In blooming good health I planned foreign trips, devised a vitamin-rich diet and bought an exercise bike. This latter acquisition provoked ribald comments from those who knew me, especially Emma who had not previously associated me with unnecessary physical activity of any kind. Jobs that could not be accomplished without the assistance of a remote control device were somehow overlooked, or farmed out to those practitioners of the black economy who would do almost anything if you paid them in cash.

I pedalled zealously for a week before incurring a pain in the peroneal nerve which confirmed me in my distaste for non-essential exercise. I limped for days and looked forward to the moment when sloth and indolence would restore me to the peak of fitness I had known before my impetuous purchase.

The customers who came into the shop this morning all seemed to be carrying book tokens received at Christmas. None had much idea about what they wanted to read. I guided them to the best-seller lists where they were relieved to discover names that they recognized.

Eventually I was able to escape to my desk where I found a verse I had started before the New Year break.

Wait, Rose, for me at the supermarket.
It's a Safe way for us to meet.

I was interrupted by the phone which is seldom a welcome call. It's a creditor, a salesman, or a customer wondering whether I have in stock Hazlitt's *Liber Amoris*, or a recent biography of Salvador Dali. (I haven't.)

'Mark Hutton Books,' I recited dolefully.

'And would that be Mark Hutton speaking?'

'It might be.'

'Mark, it's Luke Dyson.'

'Hallo,' I said, surprised. 'I've just got your Christmas card.'

'Pretty, wasn't it?'

'Why the snow? Does Australia get snow at Christmas?'

'Homesick ex-pats. They even sing "White Christmas".'

His voice had developed an Australian cadence, perhaps not surprising after living upside down for more than twenty years. 'This line is amazingly clear,' I said.

'I'm in Sussex,' Luke replied.

'That would account for it. What are you doing in Sussex? The kangaroos lose their sex appeal?'

'Nicole and I are having a trial separation. So I thought I'd fly over. You must come and have a drink with me in this grand hotel I seem to be staying in.'

'Throw in dinner and I'll be there,' I said. 'Emma's left me and I'm not much of a cook.'

'Emma's left you? You on a trial separation, too?'

'I don't think so. She left a note saying good-bye.'

While Luke made some sympathetic noises, I scribbled on my pad:

I've dumped Tess Coe
It Asda be you.

'I'm going to fill the void in your life,' Luke was saying. 'I've had an idea. You get a lot of time for ideas in Australia.'

'And "Neighbours" is all they can come up with?'

'Listen,' he said. 'We're all fifty this year.'

'Don't remind me. Who's this "we" you're talking about?'

'Our classmates. Our pals. The chaps we were at school with. Don't you ever wonder what happened to them?'

'Never,' I replied firmly.

'You're more inclined to think about the past sitting on your own in Australia. Nostalgia takes over.'

'Clearly,' I said. 'So what's the idea you've had?'

'I'm going to round up a few old classmates and invite them here to dinner.'

'And how would you do that?' I asked, confident that he was propelled by an optimism which events would show to be embarrassingly misplaced. 'You haven't seen them for thirty years.'

'You have telephone directories in this country, don't you? I'll hunt them down, no worries. You'll come, won't you?'

'I'm afraid I'm busy that night.'

'I haven't told you which night it is yet,' said Luke.

Memo to self: Don't knock Luke's crazy idea. Expose yourself to the possibility of something interesting happening.

Saturday 3 January

On the way home last night I called in on the Westacotts. Apart from anything else, I was curious about how I got back from their party.

The house had been transformed after the festivities of the New Year. The darkness had lifted, the candles extinguished, the furniture moved. The sitting-room was now an immaculate picture of gracious living, a photo from one of those magazines that the upper classes read in preference to the rude radical weeklies. The wallpaper was candy striped in purple and gray, the leisurely sofas and armchairs were enormous and the carpet was blue wool. A three-tier glass chandelier hung smugly above our heads.

Janet ushered me into this domestic showpiece with her well-practised performance of hostess although she seemed slightly bemused to see me. We sat down and faced each other across a round coffee table that had a leather centre.

'Charles is in London,' she said apologetically, as though his absence was a blow to us both. She was wearing a pink silk blouse, pale-blue trousers and golden slippers. She hadn't expected visitors.

'I suppose the opinion polls are worrying him?' I said.

'Oh, I don't think so. He's climbed the slippery pole without taking much notice of opinion polls.'

I sat in silence, suitably quashed. Janet gave me a certain look which I could translate easily. It said: What do you want? Why are you here? Explain yourself.

'The thing is,' I said, 'I seem to have mislaid my wife.'

'Mislaid her?' said Janet, looking stunned. 'How do you mean?'

'She's disappeared. The last time I saw her she was here. Which is why I've called.'

'The last time I saw her she was helping you out of the door. You seemed to be having some difficulty in standing up.'

'Oh dear,' I said. 'Is that how it was? I'm afraid New Year's Eve is a bit vague to me.'

'Well I noticed that, Mark,' said Janet who didn't look entirely happy. 'You seem to develop an abusive streak after a few drinks.'

I was being admonished here which wasn't why I had come, but I suppressed the urge to engage Janet in a little light badinage. ('Why do you dye the roots of your hair black?' was a little pleasantry that could wait.)

'Who is Rupert?' I asked. 'The last thing that I remember was that Emma was closeted with him in the conservatory.'

'Ah, Rupert,' said Janet. 'He's a lovely man and awfully rich.'

'What does he do?'

'Do? I don't think he does a lot.' Her expression made it clear that she believed it was much more commendable for people to acquire money without soiling their hands – any fool could go to work.

'Where did Emma meet him? Here?'

'Oh no. She knew him before the party. I believe they met up at that keep fit club Emma uses.'

It all made sense to me then. Emma had joined some club a few months ago with the hopeful intention of recapturing her youthful figure and, although reluctant at first, she had quickly become enthusiastic about her visits to the 'temple of torture' as she called it. Now I knew why.

When I got into my old Toyota this evening and headed for the lush opulence of Sussex I cheered myself up with the thought that if Rupert was rich I might be able to hang on to the house.

Any journey of more than forty miles is accompanied these days by a suspicion that I'll never reach my destination. My progress will be interrupted by a puncture, or a mechanical failure, or the sudden inexplicable absence of some vital fluid which the engine is apt to depend on. But I was realizing slowly that such fears were brought on by my age, and that another modern truth which had previously escaped me was that foreign cars don't break down. The Toyota behaved flawlessly.

Walton Hall Hotel was a classy place, a timber-framed fifteenth-century building with ships' timbers and log fires inside. Out the back a Tudor barn had been converted into a leisure centre with heated swimming-pool, a spa bath and a gym.

Luke Dyson stood at the bar holding a sherry. He was a short man with blond hair that showed no signs of receding and a deep sun tan, an incongruous adornment in January.

'Mark, it's great to see you,' he said, shaking my hand.

'It's good to see you,' I said. 'How can you afford to stay in a place like this?' I was curious as well as envious. The way that money clings to some people and not to others seldom has anything to do with brains, education or talent, but was more usually associated with ideas and energy. The money-makers are a separate unclassifiable breed.

'The way you make money, cobber,' said Luke, as if to a child, 'is to think of little else. In this world it's the obsessives who win, or hadn't you noticed?'

'Why don't you buy me a drink and tell me about it?' I said as he sipped his sherry.

He took the hint but surprised me by suggesting that I drink sherry too. It wasn't the potent liquid I had in mind.

He explained briskly in his clipped Australian accent, 'The falling-over liquid can wait. I'm taking you out for a little ride. I have something rather surprising to show you. We'll be back for dinner in half an hour.'

'OK,' I said. Any distraction was welcome this week. 'Tell me about money.'

'I really make a study of it. I read all the financial pages. I read books. I spend hours on the phone to my dealer in New York telling him to sell, and then more hours talking to my stockbroker in London telling him to buy. Or vice versa, or both. It's funny how the money grows. I've been bunging shiploads into the Royal Bank of Scotland in London for years. Showed great foresight as it's turned out.'

I felt slightly sick as I listened to this. Why hadn't I done something like that?

His expenditure didn't stop with the hotel. He had hired a

Porsche Boxster at the airport when he landed, and when the sherry had gone we went out and climbed into it. As we cruised over the moonlit South Downs I asked him, 'Why are you taking me for a ride in your motor-car?'

'I've made some headway,' he said proudly. 'I've reached two.'

'That's tremendous, Luke,' I said, and paused. 'Two what?'

'Spectres from our past.'

I had actually forgotten his misguided plans for some sort of reunion; any spare thinking time this week had been devoted to my vanished wife.

'Oh my God,' I said. 'Who have you unearthed?'

'Do you remember Joe Edwards? He's had gender reassignment treatment.'

'What the hell's that?'

'A sex change. He's Josephine now.'

'How did you find him in the phone book then?'

'I didn't find him. I spoke to Andrew Burrows.'

I remembered Burrows as a fat, rather boring youth who was always boasting that he would be a millionaire before he was thirty.

'Andrew told me about Jamie Croft.'

'Ah, now I am interested,' I said. 'He's the only person I was at school with who I've read about since in the newspapers.'

Jamie Croft had vowed on the day he left school that he would never work and, so far as I knew, he never had. Instead he had headed for Chelsea where a succession of rich girlfriends had provided him with a luxurious lifestyle that involved exclusive parties, foreign travel, a first acquaintance with cannabis and introduction to people in the highest social circles. His occasional appearances in the newspapers were confined to the gossip columns where he would be pictured gargling champagne, or attending a film premiere, or cavorting on a Caribbean beach with some leggy creature whose father had one title or another. It was the fathers who were the trouble. Jamie Croft was not the son-in-law they had in mind for their expensively reared darlings. BRING BACK MY DAUGHTER, PLEADS PEER was a headline I particularly remember. The girls, however, were prepared to forfeit a rich inheritance for the pleasure of Jamie's company. Not that he intended them to forfeit any inheritance. His plan was for them to bring it with them.

'He even turned up in the Australian papers from time to time,' said Luke. 'They called him the prince of the beatniks. The Aussie papers are always a little behind. It was hippies and flower power by then, wasn't it?'

'I've often wondered what happened to him,' I said. 'I always imagined that he would end up on a country estate, married to the titled daughter of some aristocrat.'

'If that's what you imagined, prepare for a shock.'

He braked suddenly, spotting a notice at the side of the road, and turned into what seemed to be a builders' yard. In one corner there was a small prefabricated shed with a yellow bike resting outside it.

'Behold,' said Luke. 'A country estate.'

'Jamie Croft lives here?' I said incredulously.

'According to Andrew Burrows. Let's knock.'

He walked across to the blue plastic door and knocked twice. From inside a sleepy voice called, 'Come in.' Luke opened the door and I followed him and looked round.

'Jesus,' I said.

It was a small, bare room with no rugs or carpets. In one corner, serving as a bed, was a mattress, and lying on it on his back with his hands behind his head was Jamie Croft. He looked slightly worn for forty-nine, a tall, lean man whom you could tell was once good-looking. He was wearing old jeans and a T-shirt, but a splendid pair of beige suede boots.

'Hallo, Jamie,' said Luke. 'Luke Dyson and Mark Hutton. You probably don't remember us.'

Jamie got up from the mattress and came to greet us. 'I remember you very well,' he said. 'How are you?'

His voice was a surprise. Without being posh it had the deep cultured tones of a BBC announcer. Perhaps it was something he had worked on.

'How are *you* seems more to the point. Is this your home?'

'I'm afraid it is.'

There was one small table with a chair. On a stand in the corner was a Primus stove, two saucepans and a plate. Beside the mattress on the floor were a few paperback books and a very small battery radio.

I pointed at a door in the corner. 'What's through there?'

'Just a loo and a sink.'

'Cripes,' said Luke. 'Andrew Burrows said you were short of money but this ... this is penury.'

'Penury?' said Jamie with a hollow laugh. 'Penury is something I aspire to.'

'You're wearing a wonderful pair of boots,' I said. My remark carried the implication that his finances were in better shape than he was telling us, but his reply promptly dispatched such an unworthy suspicion.

'I found them in a skip.'

'What do you live on?' Luke asked.

'I get forty-five pounds income support from the state which is very good of them as I've never given them a penny. I live off that.'

'How?'

'You learn to do without. My needs are very small. I've got a second-hand bike that I bought on hire purchase over eighteen months. I cycle down to the supermarket at the end of the day when they sell off cheap the stuff they're not going to get rid of.'

'And what do you eat?' I asked.

'Well, it's not scrambled duck eggs and caviar blinis any more. I live on brown rice and pasta mostly.'

There was a profound silence as this bleak news sank in. We couldn't sit down as there was only one chair, so we stood there awkwardly with Luke shaking his head sadly and me wondering how a life could go so spectacularly wrong.

'What happened to all that affluent crumpet?' I asked. 'The poor little rich girls who queued up for a bonk? You were supposed to wander off into the sunset with one of them on your arm and her chequebook in your pocket.'

'It wasn't that calculated,' Jamie protested. 'I fell in love with half of them. But the parental opposition was ferocious. They saw me as a penniless fortune hunter.'

'I can't understand that,' I said.

'You don't know much about the upper classes,' he replied, ignoring my irony. 'They didn't steal all that land three hundred years ago to give it away now. Least of all to me.'

'So?'

'So I got older, the women disappeared and I had no job or money. It came as a bit of a shock. I had been living so well. I've travelled all over the world, usually first class.'

'And now ... this.'

'And now this. But I've nearly lost interest in money. I like to eat, and that's about it. Someone once said "Fate can't harm me today because I've eaten". I thought I was going to end up married to money and living a life of splendour, but I've no desire for that now. I've met some very wealthy people with huge homes that are full of valuable things, but the moment you have stuff like that it becomes a burden. You have to look after it, or pay someone to look after it, insure it and worry about it. It's like carrying a rock around on your back.'

'That's one way of looking at it,' I said.

'From my perspective it's the only way to look at it,' said Jamie. 'What brings you chaps round here, anyway?'

'Ah yes,' said Luke. 'An invitation to dinner. I'm organizing a little reunion get-together with some people who were in our class at school.'

'Food?' said Jamie. 'Meat, vegetables and wine? I'll come.'

Memo to self: When you win the Lottery make out the first cheque to Jamie Croft.

Monday 5 January

Why has my wife left her shoes behind? I have just counted thirty-four pairs of them, neatly stacked in her wardrobe. The Imelda Marcos of Trebor Avenue.

In fact I made a tour of the house to see what is left here of hers. There's quite a lot. Does this mean she's coming back?

Apart from the clothes, the dresses, the jackets and skirts and the blouses that hang on her fancy coat-hangers, there's a battery of cosmetics in the bathroom that I thought she regarded as essential: bath relaxer, beauty fluid, nail polish remover (but no nail polish), revitalizing shampoo, self-tanning cream, baby powder, hair colourant, body lotion, avocado oil handcream, an energizing composition. How can she be living without it?

There are also treasured pieces of furniture which she bought herself to enhance the quality of her life: a leather-bound safari chest, a three-drawer sideboard, a wooden music centre on which she could play her old 78s as well as her new CDs, a ceramic lamp hand painted in Chinese royal blue, and a handmade wing-backed armchair upholstered in Italian leather which she thought would impress visitors. Doesn't she want these things?

I had a dream last night which was probably induced by Luke Dyson's determination to drag some of us back into the past. But instead of dreaming about the classmates that he's trying to assemble, I dreamt about Marisa Wynn – same age, same era, different school. At seventeen we were wrapped in an affair so frenzied and wanton that I limped home from our dates with aches in places that I had not previously used. There was a mutual enthusiasm in which the heart bypassed the brain, and epic couplings took place in green fields watched by curious rabbits who thought they had a monopoly on that sort of thing. There were also, to ring the changes, vertical trysts against spider-plagued haystacks when I achieved heights I have not known since.

Afterwards we would lie sated in a field that was redolent with the aromas of the countryside and discuss our future. Marisa was a very pretty girl with black hair and blue eyes and, like most girls of her age at that time, she wanted to get married. It was far too early for the idea to appeal to me. I was still looking for a career and my father had arranged for me to spend six months with his sister in Canada where he thought that various lucrative projects might emerge.

Two letters from Marisa arrived in Vancouver and then they stopped abruptly. By the time I flew home, disillusioned with Canada, her family had moved. I gave up women altogether and devoted myself first to accountancy and then to the shop. As far as I could see the emancipation of women had been followed immediately by the emasculation of men and I shied away from the restrictions that marriage would impose.

There was for a year a jolly girl called Bryony who came into the shop to flirt, but she vanished when she realized that there was no hope of a wedding. From time to time she wrote to let me know that she was still available. In a nod towards my own attempts at comic verse, her last message had been moodily poetic:

To keep you informed, I'm living in Slough.
The man I was with found another.
'All men are bastards' is what I say now,
So I'm back home and living with Mother.

Concerned that her verse was better than mine, I never replied.

Memo to self: I wonder who Marisa is sharing a duvet with these days?

Thursday 8 January

One of the more unwelcome moments in my working life comes when the bookshop is invaded by an author. They come in as if they own the place, scan the shelves for their books and then rearrange them so that the cover is displayed instead of just the spine. Given the chance, they'll grill you on sales. You could break the hearts of these curiously vulnerable creatures by giving them the facts. They have emerged blinking from their frowsty studies with very little idea about what is going on in the real world, and then watch disbelievingly as customers come in and buy books written by somebody else.

Today's visitor was Jonathan W. Potts, that acclaimed author of whimsical paperbacks which have acquired a coterie of fans among those readers who weren't quite ready for Umberto Eco or Gabriel Garcia Marquez. His latest attempt to replace the nation's scowl with a grin was called *I Keep Forgetting I've Got Alzheimers* which, perhaps due to his tireless promotion, was now loitering at the bottom end of the top twenty. Certainly the customers who came into the shop today would be buying his embarrassing attempt at humour because this was a signing session, advertised in the window. In fact there was already a queue that stretched into the street when the author, who was all height and no width and dressed in an unflattering brown check suit, ducked through the door and rushed at me like a man with no time to waste. 'How many copies have you got?' he asked. 'There's a horde out there.'

'We have enough,' I promised, and escorted him to a table and chair at the front of the shop which were always brought out and dusted on these occasions. (The last occupant of the chair, a diffident woman who wrote about cats, caused congestion in the street.)

My lady upstairs, the ebullient Mrs Pringle, who was drawn to celebrity like a fly to dung, had insisted on coming down to preside over the event – to take the money, provide the change and attend to the whims and requirements of Jonathan W. Potts. I was glad to let her do it. I thought he had been exalted far beyond the position his talent deserved, but in these difficult days shifting books needed help and for some reason I had never been able to fathom the author's signature on a copy was a great help in shifting it.

I retired to my hidey-hole to look at a paper, but Mrs Pringle appeared almost immediately to announce that Jonathan W. Potts would like a whisky. I dealt with this from a bottle that was kept for just such an eventuality, and then looked down at the pad which I was slowly filling with verse.

Our farmer who lives in Devon
Harold be thy name.

I crossed this out and tried a better one.

I'll tell you why
She rejected your suit
She's bespoken for.

I was thinking about another one when Luke came in. Alone among today's customers he walked straight past the Jonathan W. Potts show and headed for my corner.

'Who's that?' he asked.

'That's Jonathan W. Potts.'

'What *the* Jonathan W. Potts?'

'Have you heard of him?'

'No. Listen, I've been to France through the Channel Tunnel.'

I found this news strangely depressing. It would be months or even years before I got round to enjoying the sunless delights of the Channel Tunnel, but once these people started travelling there was no holding them. Whole continents were devoured in days.

'Fantastic,' I muttered. 'Did you enjoy it?'

'No. The view was terrible.'

He was looking at the whisky bottle on my desk so I offered him a drink. 'You're supposed to write a book before you can have Scotch in this establishment, but I'll make an exception in your case.'

He took the drink gratefully and said, 'I've found Paul Ross. I was waiting for the train so went through a phone book that covered the area. I've got into the habit now. Show me a phone book and I'll scour it for names from the past.'

'Most people would use the Friends Reunited site on the Web.'

'I tried that. There wasn't a single name I knew.'

'Paul Ross,' I said. 'Wasn't he the chap who was going to be a vet?'

We were interrupted by Mrs Pringle who wanted more books. I opened two boxes that each contained twenty-four copies and carried them out to the table.

'Well timed,' said Jonathan W. Potts. 'Any more whisky?' The queue seemed to be longer than it was before so I refilled his glass.

'Yes,' said Luke, when I finally sat down again. 'Paul Ross was going to be a vet. I didn't find out what happened. I just invited him to dinner. I've fixed it for Monday, by the way. The hotel manager is going to give us a room of our own.'

'And how many will be there?' I asked.

'Five at the moment with Andrew Burrows. Of course I may have found somebody else by then.'

'Andrew Burrows was the future millionaire?'

'He was the guy who knew how to shake the money tree. Always wheeling and dealing. Buying in one antique shop and selling at a profit in another.'

'Well let's hope he made it. He might give us some.'

Luke gave me a funny look which mocked my optimism. 'I don't think so. If millionaires gave money away they wouldn't be millionaires. He sounded terrible, by the way. He'd just been to a funeral. Anyway, he's coming to the dinner, and Monday night's the night.'

'Book now to ensure disappointment,' I said.

Memo to self: Stop being snide ('maliciously derogatory' according to my dictionary). You haven't got many friends left.

Saturday 10 January

Things are looking up. Charles Westacott has been deselected. Apparently he has spent less time in his constituency in the last two years than any MP in Britain. The local Labour activists, understandably miffed, are going to find a new candidate who actually shows up.

Janet is distraught. I bumped into her in the food aisles at Marks & Spencer where she was looking for a lot of smoked salmon and I was looking for one prawn cocktail. She talked of 'the ingratitude of the masses' and the 'flaws in democracy'.

'What will happen?' I asked.

'There's talk of a seat in the House of Lords.'

This is the worst news of all. She would become Lady Westacott!

'That would be wonderful,' I said.

My capacity for duplicity is bottomless. Perhaps I should become an MP. There's a vacancy coming up, I hear, in the north.

Monday 12 January

When I reached the Walton Hall Hotel in my best pale-blue suit Luke had already collected Jamie from his shed. This wasn't quite the selfless gesture it seemed; Luke wanted to check that Jamie would be dressed appropriately for dinner in a fashionable hotel. In the event he was still wearing jeans and the boots he had found in a skip, but he had also put on a smart white shirt. He could pass for an Italian film producer.

'What time did you tell these reprobates to show?' I asked Luke, as he handed me a whisky.

'Seven-thirty for eight,' he said, consulting a Rolex. 'I suppose we can count on the bastards to be late.' He had been to the Royal Bank of Scotland in London that afternoon to check on how much money he had casually diverted to them over the years and what the interest had raised it to. He was delighted to find that it was £90,000.

The bar was filled with a pre-dinner crowd whose bills were no doubt being paid by their employers. They looked like a mixture of salesmen, insurance executives, company directors and soaring stars in one industry or another who had business to attend to in this verdant corner of the globe. Their apparent affluence depressed me as I considered the advantages of not being self-employed.

I was suddenly aware that a tall, heavy man in a dark suit was standing beside us. He had short black hair and a small moustache, like a homosexual in the 1990s. His sad, tired eyes did not suggest that he had enjoyed a life of uninterrupted triumph.

'Andrew Burrows,' he said solemnly.

'Burrows the money man!' said Luke enthusiastically. 'Let me buy you a drink.'

'A whisky.' Andrew Burrows looked at me and then at Jamie Croft. 'I recognize you,' he said. 'I've seen your picture in the papers.'

'Don't believe everything you read in them,' said Jamie. 'This gentleman here is Mark Hutton.'

'Of course,' said Andrew Burrows. 'I should have recognized you. Still a good-looking sort of chap.'

'I do my best,' I said.

Luke returned with the whisky. 'Unless I'm very much mistaken that man coming in is Paul Ross.'

The final member of our group strolled across the bar towards us. Plump but tidy, he was wearing a dark-blue blazer with grey flannels and a pink shirt with a foulard instead of a tie. He had a distant look in his eyes like those of a mystic who is trying to create the impression that he knows things that you don't.

Luke, now thoroughly engrossed in the role of host, reintroduced him to us all and offered him a drink.

'A mineral water,' he said. 'I don't touch alcohol.'

When he had bought it, Luke suggested that we all move with our drinks to our very own dining-room where a round table for five had been laid near the window which provided a pleasant view of the large grounds at the back of the hotel which included a small lake. At the centre of our table were carnations.

A waiter appeared almost immediately and took a unanimous order for roast beef except for Paul Ross who turned out to be a vegetarian as well as teetotal and opted for spaghetti.

'Half the world starving and the other half slimming,' he said enigmatically. 'There's a sense of guilt which cradle Catholics never entirely lose.' When the food arrived, along with half-a-dozen bottles of wine, we suddenly realized that he was saying grace.

'I can't wait to ask,' said Luke, when we had started the meal, 'did you make your piles, Andrew?'

'Piles? I got haemorrhoids, if that's any good to you.'

'You were going to be a millionaire before you were thirty,' I reminded him.

He nodded in reluctant recognition of this ancient boast. 'I did make a lot of money and then I lost it. I was made bankrupt last year.'

'Christ,' said Luke. 'How did you make it in the first place?'

'Nursing homes for pensioners. At one time I had twenty of them. Then the Labour government set up a commission to investigate the concept of nursing homes and the whole thing began to come apart at the seams. In the end the tax man did me and I lost everything.'

This wasn't the message that Luke was expecting to hear and he shook his head in disbelief.

'One day we'll all have to wear helmets and insert pound coins if we want to breathe,' said Andrew.

'What about you, Paul?' I said. 'How are the animals?'

'Animals?'

'Vets deal with animals, don't they? That's what I heard.'

'Oh that. I'm afraid I didn't make it. I went into insurance but was made redundant a couple of years ago.'

'So you've retired?'

'Not exactly. I'm a part-time traffic warden.'

This news had a curiously deflating effect on Luke who seemed to sink in his chair.

'Don't worry,' said Paul Ross, who had noticed this. 'I expect Jamie's extra-curricular activities have produced a country mansion and a Bentley.'

'He's got a bike and lives in a shed,' said Luke. 'What's the matter with us?'

'A bike?' said Paul Ross. 'I'm very impressed. Environmentally sound and very healthy for you.'

'Very dangerous for me, actually,' Jamie said. 'Imperious ladies in Range Rovers knock me off without noticing. The revenge of the upper classes! But the last time I came off was because my hands and arms wouldn't do what my brain was telling them. I thought I'd had a stroke, but my doctor told me that it was a neural problem not uncommon among people who did LSD in their youth.'

'I think we'll skip over your pharmaceutical misdemeanours if you don't mind,' said Paul Ross. 'I disapprove of that sort of thing.'

Jamie ignored him. 'Purple hearts and pot! Those were the days. Now it's Prozac. Still, it makes boring people interesting, I suppose. You should try it, Paul.'

I refilled my glass with red wine and then looked to see what I was drinking. Not surprisingly it was a wine from

Australia, lovingly chosen by our host: a Cabernet Sauvignon 'full of moss, tobacco and cedar flavours' according to a baffling label on the back.

Luke, recovering from the bad news, tried to revitalize the table with a subject snatched from thin air. He made an unfortunate choice.

'So what have you been up to, Andrew? You sounded a bit down when I talked to you on the phone.'

'I'd been to a funeral, hadn't I?'

'Ah yes. Whose?'

'It's too depressing to talk about.'

'Fine,' said Luke, but Andrew Burrows, helped by the wine, actually wanted to talk. He drank half a glass and stared out of the window.

'It was my brother, William,' he said. 'A total mental collapse. You could see what brought it on. A rancorous marriage, a failed career. For some weeks he just sat in a chair and didn't talk very much except that every half-hour or so he would say "Bollocks". Then one day he slipped out. He was found wandering round Tesco's in his underpants, making strange animal noises. The doctor said he was trying to tell us something.'

'That he needed a new pair of trousers, perhaps,' said Jamie, but to our credit nobody laughed.

'The following week he drove his Volkswagen into a wood, fixed a rubber hose to the exhaust and killed himself. It was a rather unusual suicide.'

'It's quite common actually,' I said.

'The difference in William's case was that he was scared he would change his mind, so he superglued his hands to the steering wheel. They had to cut it off, and his body was lifted out of the car still clutching the wheel.'

The grotesque scene which this evoked guaranteed a further

silence. The conversational topics that were floating to the surface in this room did not seem likely to engender the gaiety that Luke had hoped for. Sadly conscious of this, he struggled to alter the mood. He had convened this gathering in the hope of some light-hearted banter and a few laughs, but a pall of gloom was beginning to hover over the table. He amused them by telling them how Emma had left me with a note stuck to my forehead.

'You're lucky,' said Andrew Burrows, who had now drunk at least one of the bottles of wine. 'Do you know what Shirley cost me when I had money?'

'Would that be Shirley Appleton?' Luke asked. 'I used to fancy her.'

'You wouldn't recognize her now,' said Andrew. 'She looks like Marilyn Monroe. It began with a nose job in 1991. Two and half grand. Then came silicone implants that took her breast size from 32A to 34DD. Another two and half grand, and the same again for liposuction. Finally there was a teeth job that cost three grand. Over ten thousand pounds, and what have I got for it?'

'Something pretty special, I should think,' suggested Luke.

'It turned me. I'm gay now.'

He looked defiantly round the room ready to deal with any ribald comments that came his way but people were too surprised to say anything.

It was at this point that Paul Ross dropped his little bombshell. He looked directly at me across the table and said, 'By the way, Marisa sends her love.'

I looked down at the table, strewn as it was with empty wine bottles, discarded food on plates that had yet to be removed, and screwed-up napkins.

'What?' I said, confused.

'Marisa sends her love,' he repeated.

'Marisa Wynn?'

'No. Marisa Ross.'

I fell silent for a moment, struggling to come to terms with the idea that Marisa had got herself attached to this sanctimonious creep, but then I remembered that he had fancied her all those years ago when she was mine. I remembered an occasion when he had boasted to her about the money that he was going to earn as a vet, but he was made to sound foolish because at that age girls weren't interested in money.

'How is she?' I asked. 'I didn't know you'd married her.'

'You'd gone to Canada to make your fortune. And she's fine.'

He must have moved quickly, I thought, if they were married before I got home. But I could see now why the letters had suddenly stopped.

The waiter had appeared to collect plates and bottles, and a second one followed him brandishing menus. Outside, swans had appeared from somewhere and were patrolling the lake as if they owned it. The waiter reappeared with a tray of desserts that seemed to be mostly pistachio and almond ice cream, and asked how many wanted coffee. When this information, with its various finicky variations, had been passed along, I turned back to Paul Ross.

'Any kids?' I asked.

'Kids?' he said. 'I'm a grandfather. Where did my life go! What happened to Ford Cortinas, Brigitte Bardot and Six-Five Special?'

'A grandfather?' said Luke. 'You're kidding.'

Paul Ross, his reputation impugned, plunged a hand into his blazer pocket and produced a photograph that was passed round the table. It was a colour snap taken in a garden. It showed Paul standing alongside a man of about thirty who was holding a baby, the three-generation shot that looked so warm-hearted behind the right frame.

When the picture reached me I found that I was looking at a

picture of myself. The man of thirty looked exactly as I had looked at that age. It was evidently not a resemblance that Paul Ross had noticed.

'What are their names?' I asked.

'My grandson is Samuel. My son, oddly enough, is called Mark. It was Marisa's idea and I went along with it. She obviously liked your name.'

I took another look at the picture and then passed it to Luke. 'What is she doing these days?' I asked.

'Helping the sagging family income by working in an art gallery.'

'Oh really?' I said. 'Which art gallery would that be?'

'Picture This in Soho. Owned by some barmy lord.'

I slipped off to the gentlemen's washroom, as this splendid hotel called the bog, and made a note of the name. My mind was in turmoil. I was joined a moment later by Luke whose expression was distinctly rueful.

'I seem to have blown the thick end of four hundred quid on this feast, and what have we got? The millionaire-to-be is a gay bankrupt. The would-be vet is a part-time traffic warden with a funny look in his eyes. And the man who expected to inherit a stately home is dossing in a shed. Are we talking about blasted dreams, or what?'

'It's not a good record,' I admitted. 'Perhaps we should blame the school.'

'I forgot to say that another man who had a head full of dreams is making ends meet by flogging the mind-stretching works of Jeffrey Archer. How do you make a living? Did you know that only one person in ten has ever been into a proper bookshop? I read that in a newspaper.'

I put my hand on his shoulder.

'Did you know that one father in ten unknowingly brings up a child who isn't his? I read that in a newspaper, too.'

Memo to self: Take in some culture. A visit to an art gallery would improve your mood.

Saturday 17 January

My in-laws are outlaws. They moved four years ago to the Isle of Man, and I don't think it was cats without tails, motorbikes or birching that attracted them. They live in the land of the alluring tax loophole. This was no doubt appropriate given the bizarre range of Mr Benson's investments, most of which were a mystery to me.

I rang him up. His attitude to me had always registered disappointment rather than hostility. Initially he was curious about the bookshop and seemed to welcome into his family an imagined infusion of culture to counteract the endless scrutiny of balance sheets; but when this cultural enterprise failed to produce the financial rewards that he regarded, no doubt rightly, as necessary, he seemed to lose his enthusiasm, particularly when the failure was compounded by the non-appearance of grandchildren.

'Is Emma there?' I asked.

'I believe she is, Mark,' he said. 'Hang on.'

But the voice that eventually returned to the phone was his, not hers.

'I'm afraid she's out,' he said. 'She's filming.'

'She's what?' I said.

'Filming.'

'I'm not sure I got that,' I said, baffled.

'You're not keeping up with the news, Mark. The Isle of Man is now the film-making capital of the UK. We made nine films here last year. Colin Firth, Kenneth Branagh. They get a quarter of the budget from the film commission here. It's not charity. It fills hotels, restaurants, planes.'

'And what is there to film?'

'We've got the best of the UK. You ought to get out more. One moment you're in the Yorkshire Dales, then you come round a bend and there's the Cornish coastline.'

'And Emma's filming something?'

'Well, I've invested in the project, which helped.'

Jesus Christ, my wife's going to be a film star.

When she came into my shop eighteen years ago she was a twenty year old with a similar dream. In fact the book she had come in to buy was *The World Encyclopaedia of Film*. Now she was thirty-eight and the dream had moved closer. In my long years of struggle in the bookshop she had shown no interest in getting a job no matter how dire our financial situation became. Occasionally, I suspected, a cheque arrived from her father; I didn't care to ask.

Emma's interest was confined to an amateur dramatic society which she joined and then helped to run. Once a year she would turn up on stage in some small hall, giving us a taste of Ayckbourn, Frayn or Oscar Wilde. I found it rather sad. If you needed an audience you wanted a larger one than was assembled here.

Now it looked as if she was about to find one. A mysterious combination of serendipity, paternal investment and domestic flight had dropped her in the right place to display her talents to a larger audience than you would find in a hall.

'How is she doing?' I asked.

'Very well, apparently,' said Mr Benson. 'But she's always had the talent.'

'She should have gone to drama school.'

'There were plans in that direction but then she married you at twenty which rather threw a spanner in the works.'

The rebuke came across the ether like an arrow but I didn't respond. My recollection was that our marriage was at

Emma's insistence and at thirty-two was becoming too old to resist.

Mr Benson cleared his throat. 'Have you and Emma split up?' he asked.

'You tell me,' I said.

Memo to self: Wait for the video.

Sunday 18 January

Sundays are empty now. It is often midday before I can drag myself from my bed and keep my dutiful appointment with the newspapers. But today I decided on a more positive approach to my only day off. I got up, had a shower, cooked breakfast and then jumped in the Toyota and headed for Luke's hotel in Sussex.

The receptionist, a short blonde girl with a cavernous bosom which seriously confused me this early on a Sunday morning, made a phone call and then turned back to me with a radiant smile. 'Mr Dyson said would you go up? He's in 212.'

Mr Dyson had already opened the door for me and was now lying back on a sofa in the window with his feet, in a pair of bright check socks, some inches higher than his head.

'I could get used to this,' he said. 'In fact I've booked in for another month.'

I sank into a luxurious armchair. 'Is that a coffee machine I see over there?'

'I catch your drift,' he said, getting up. When he'd made us both a coffee, he announced, 'I've had another idea.'

My heart sank a little at this news. I was content with the daily equilibrium and would prefer it to be undisturbed by Luke's novel suggestions, fraught as they were with meetings I didn't want and social occasions I could do without.

'You don't need ideas any more, Luke. You're in England. We've got television sets.'

'No, listen,' he said. 'We hold another dinner here, but this time we invite one of our old teachers. Who educated us? Who made us what we are? We had five disasters at dinner the other night. Let's bring in somebody who was responsible and show them what they achieved.'

'It would have to be Thacker,' I said, remembering our vicious and destructive form master. 'Would we be allowed to beat him up?'

'Be my guest,' said Luke, but he was interrupted by the surprisingly shrill demand of the room phone. He got up to answer it. 'Send him up,' he said. He put the phone down and turned to me. 'It's Jamie Croft. Is Sunday morning visiting a British tradition?'

'It's not one that I encourage,' I told him, but he was already crossing the room to open the door. Jamie came in wearing a dirty blue T-shirt and jeans. The splendid boots were still in place.

'Hallo, people,' he said. 'I knew that if I cycled this far there would probably be somebody who would buy me a drink.'

'Luke's just had another idea,' I told him. 'Creative little sod, isn't he?'

'What's this one?' Jamie asked warily.

'We have another dinner, but this time we invite Thacker as well.'

'Thacker the whacker? I'd sooner meet a paranoid psychotic in a dark alleyway. Why would I want to break bread with that vindictive shit?'

'Revenge, Jamie,' said Luke. 'Who knocked the confidence out of us with a cane? Who thought he was subduing a bunch of no-hopers when he was in fact creating them?'

'Kids come out of Eton full of confidence and end up

running the country,' I said. 'Our lot were cowed. They knew their place and it was never going to be in the bloody Cabinet.'

Jamie took the coffee that Luke offered him. 'You've persuaded me,' he said. 'Bring the bastard on and I'll dismantle him. Let's get to him before his faculties unravel.'

'When we've sorted him out we can move on to the others,' said Luke. 'Do you remember that English teacher Harry Lay who couldn't even conjugate his own surname?'

'I remember being taught that Rangoon was the capital of Burma,' I said. 'Now it's not called Rangoon and it's not called Burma. What a waste of time that was.'

'Are seven sevens still forty-nine or has there been some edict from Brussels?' Jamie asked.

A mood of disillusionment settled on the room. The past produced endless scenes in which time had either been abused or wasted. The group of fiscal under-achievers gathered here began to feel resentment.

'He should be attached by a thick chain to a large immovable object,' Jamie declared.

'Who should?'

'Arnold Thacker.'

'Arnold. Was that his name?'

'That was the bastard,' said Jamie. 'Arnold Thacker.'

Luke had moved on from all this and was covering his bright check socks with an expensive pair of black suede shoes.

'I'm taking you down to the bar to buy you a beer,' he announced. Once we had established ourselves there, pints of lager in hand, it became clear why Jamie had cycled over.

'The thing is,' he said, 'I could utilize some wonga.'

'What language is he talking?' asked Luke. 'I only do Anglo-Oz.'

'I think he wants some money,' I said.

'Money, Jamie?' said Luke. 'You don't use money. Your frugality is an example to us all.'

'They've cut off the electricity,' Jamie told him. 'No lights.' I felt sorry for him. Behind the smiling social confidence that had brought him triumphantly through several hundred society shindigs there now lurked a destitute failure.

Luke was already producing his wallet. 'How much do you need?'

Jamie looked at the wad of notes displayed in the wallet. 'Two hundred would do it.'

Luke peeled off ten twenties and handed them across. 'You can pay me back when your ship comes in. That's what they used to say, isn't it?'

'I believe it is,' I said, imagining the prolonged wait on some windswept jetty that Jamie would have to endure before any money arrived for his pocket.

Memo to self: Why can't you hand over £200 to a friend without even noticing it?

Friday 23 January

Charles Westacott comes into the shop for only the third time since I opened. It's Friday, and few MPs show up in Westminster on a Friday. He seems to be remarkably jaunty for a man who is about to be booted out of the House of Commons.

'Hiya, Mark!' he says with an uncharacteristic display of affability. 'I've got a little order for you.' He produces an immaculate sheet of paper from his inside pocket on which he has written the titles of half -a-dozen books. They include, I see at a glance, *Who's Who*, a history of the House of Lords and *Debrett*.

'I was sorry to hear you've been deselected,' I tell him with what remorse I can muster.

'Oh, don't worry about that,' he replies, stroking his little moustache. 'I'm going to fix the bastards.'

'Fix them?' I say. 'How will you do that?'

'They thought I'd go quietly at the next election and let their new man inherit the seat. No way! I'm resigning the seat now to make them fight a by-election. They'll lose the seat to the Lib-Dems on current form!'

'The PM won't like that, will he?' I suggest.

'With his majority he's not worried. He hates the bastards as much as I do. They're all to the left of Joe Stalin.'

It is clear that Charles Westacott is not a man to mess with.

'I'll deliver the books to your house,' I tell him. 'How's Janet?'

'Looking forward to her elevation. Any news of Emma?'

'I haven't heard a word since she left. What elevation?'

He winks at me and touches his nose. 'Have a look at the books I've ordered. You'll get the picture.'

He is about to leave when I remember a question I have for him. 'That chap Rupert who was at your party.'

'What about him?'

'Is he anything to do with the movies?'

'He's a film director if that counts.'

'Never heard of him,' I say.

'Well he made *The Donkey Tree* which was an Oscar nominee, I believe.'

'Good for him,' I mutter as Charles leaves with a cheery wave.

There are two customers devouring one of the new novels without having to find money, and I shuffle round the shop examining the stock. I am immersed in one of Updike's *Rabbit* novels when Mrs Pringle comes in.

'Mrs Pringle!' I say. 'I've been looking for you.'

'I went to stay with my sister for a few days.'

'That's nice,' I say. 'Now what are you doing on Monday?'

'Looking after the shop?'

'You've got it in one,' I tell her.

Memo to self: I seem to be writing in the present tense today. It's the influence of the *Rabbit* book.

Monday 26 January

I drove north towards the Thames like a minor character in a Bond movie. On the seat beside me were a pair of dark glasses and a pale-blue baseball cap with SYDNEY 2000 on the front which somebody had left in the shop. I was confident that these two items would successfully conceal my identity.

I had left the indefatigable Mrs Pringle in charge of the shop. Monday is one of the busier days because the reading public has spent the weekend submerged in newspapers and supplements that have whetted their appetites for the latest productions from the publishers' never-ending conveyor belts. But I knew that Mrs Pringle could handle it; she diligently reads the same supplements herself.

It only took half an hour to park the Toyota – halfway to heaven in a multi-storey – and I was reminded of why my visits to London were both reluctant and rare. I put on the dark glasses and the baseball cap and headed for the street, hoping that I looked like an eccentric tourist.

Taxis tootled past carrying, I imagined, respectable citizens towards extravagant scenes of unbridled debauchery, but despite its raffish image Soho has a more serious side. Marx wrote *Das Kapital* here, international film companies had their offices packed into the tiny streets. And there were art galleries.

Picture This was tucked between a clothes designer's workshop and an Italian baker. At first I walked past it, hardly daring to look in. It wasn't part of my plan today to talk to Marisa because I would soon be having another dinner with Paul Ross and I didn't want to hear what he thought about my dropping in to see his wife. But I wanted to see her.

A poster in the window revealed that the current exhibition featured a Japanese woman artist who according to the photograph had uncharacteristically round, staring eyes. Her speciality seemed to be to paint polka dots on every available surface, walls, ceilings, bodies. She favoured black polka dots on yellow, and red on blue.

I had the impression as I walked by that there was a woman in the gallery but I couldn't stop to stare. It wasn't like a shop window where a passer-by could stop and study the goods. I went some way up the street and then turned back. This time I was lucky. A beggar stopped me as I was outside the gallery and I was able to stand there while I fiddled in my pocket for a pound coin. I took some time over this – the beggar was in no hurry – and I saw Marisa as she turned and came across to one of the polka dot paintings. She was wearing a short black dress that made her look about twenty.

I always knew that she had the type of face that wouldn't age much, and the hair was still jet black and the eyes bright. Only her figure had put on a little weight. She looked at me now, curious about the financial negotiations on the pavement. Or had she recognized me through the disguise?

I thrust the coin at the beggar, moved on quickly and turned into the next pub for a whisky. The sheer availability of Marisa – I could walk in and talk to her at any time – filled me with hope, and the glorious way she had survived the years was better than I had ever dreamed.

Wednesday 28 January

The way they pronounce daughter
Means laughter should be lorter
And cough is cow
To rhyme with bough
While from the tap comes waughter

Another busy day in the office then. Sometimes I saw myself as a cultural missionary in a commercial bazaar where every till rang more often than mine.

The customers come in, of course, drawn to the glossy new volumes that only appeared that week, but handing over the amount of money that books cost these days seemed to present technical problems that they couldn't overcome. I once had a customer who read all six volumes of Churchill's war memoirs while standing in the shop. He even left his bookmark in when he went home. Impressed by the man's effrontery, I couldn't quite bring myself to protest.

Today I had a man who wanted every single novel that Graham Greene had written, which was a nice little order if I could assemble it. Unfortunately Greene withdrew his second and third novels, refusing to have them reissued, and it would take a trawl through obscure magazines or second-hand shops to discover copies. The next customer, a bearded youth, spent some time describing the contents of a novel whose title he couldn't remember. He was so familiar with the story that you began to wonder why he wanted the book at all.

'It's *Stepping Westward* by Malcolm Bradbury,' I told him. 'There's a paperback over there.' He collected the book gratefully and brought it back to me to pay. He obviously thought I was a genius, but when you spend all day surrounded by books you pick things up.

The next arrival was Luke.

'I've been buying things,' he said. 'Clothes, shoes. I arrived in this country with very little and needed to replenish my wardrobe.'

'Coffee?' I asked.

'What I really want is to use your phone. I haven't had time to phone Thacker yet.'

We went to the back of the shop where I provided him with a phone and three directories.

'I sent an e-mail to Nicole,' he said. 'I thought I'd better let her know where I am in case she's ill or something.'

'Did she answer?'

He shook his head. 'Do you hear from Emma?'

'Not a word. Funny the way our wives left us both without a hint of regret. Quite hurtful, really.'

'I blame Thacker,' said Luke. 'I blame him for everything now. I've got into the habit. He knocked the tenderness out of us.' He plunged into the first directory like an expert, and his finger ran down the pages at impressive speed, and then suddenly stopped.

'Found the sod,' he said, and started to chant 'I know where you live!'

He dialled the number and I picked up my other phone to listen to the conversation. The voice dutifully reciting his number came back to me with its whining intimidatory inflection and nasal pitch. I still expected to hear a derisive sneer or a puerile attempt at sarcasm.

'Mr Thacker?' Luke asked.

'Speaking.'

'Mr Thacker, I'm Luke Dyson. I was a pupil of yours in the late sixties. A few of us from that class have recently had a small reunion, and we decided to ask whether you'd care to join us for dinner one evening. As our guest.'

Mr Thacker took some time to assimilate this information. 'Who did you say you were?'

'Luke Dyson.'

'Are you Australian?'

'No, I just spent some time there.'

'Well it would be very pleasant to join you and your friends for dinner. I don't get a lot of invitations these days.'

'Do you know the Walton Hall Hotel?'

'Indeed I do.'

'Would Monday at eight be all right?'

'I don't have to consult an appointment book these days. That would be fine.'

'And would you need a lift?'

'I'm only sixty-five Mr Dyson. I can still drive a car. Are we going to talk over old times?'

'We certainly are,' said Luke. He replaced the phone, jumped up and punched the air.

'Arnold Thacker – it's payback time!'

Memo to self: I don't feel entirely happy about this.

FEBRUARY

February is a chilly interval before
the world starts again.
– *Sean Hunt*

Sunday 1 February

If I could have my life over again I would have far more sex. How many orgasms did I miss because I was doing something else that was less interesting? How many willing girls have wandered away unsatisfied and confused because I was playing darts or drinking beer? It is true that when I was young sex was not as available as it is today. At school they thought you would end up in court if you touched a girl's breasts. Today you get dumped if you don't.

Sex is in the air, on the air and in the streets. It's the year of the bare midriff which I find surprisingly erotic. I suppose it is because midriffs have previously been covered up. Men are funny like that. If ears had been concealed for a hundred years and were suddenly on display males would be lurching around London with erections like baseball bats distorting the shape of their trousers.

I can see now that from the age of around eighteen I should have been shagging anything that moved. What on earth was I doing with my time that would have been better than that? There were periods of my life, post-Marisa, when I didn't have any sex at all. Who did I think I was? The Pope? The underuse of the available faculties is a sin that I regret; the delights that I neglected fill me with shame. The celibate is a disfigured creature.

I should have devoted myself to the treats while the opportunities were there. It shouldn't even have mattered whether the girl was pretty. Legs, breasts, buttocks – there was a feast continually on offer and mostly I failed to take advantage of it. I strolled round discussing Wilson or Watergate when I could have been tearing the pants off an eager young lady with all the correct appetites who was waiting for me to come alive. I could weep.

What has brought these thoughts on?

Partly, I suppose, it is the fact that I now live alone. Frustration is endemic. Another reason is that although it is Sunday I have resisted the urge to drive down to Luke's hotel for more of the invigorating lager as I am heading that way tomorrow for an unwelcome assignation with Arnold Thacker. Instead I have stayed at home and reintroduced myself to the Hoover before settling down with the Sunday papers which manage to suggest in their artless way that most people are getting laid four times a week in three different positions with two versatile lovers. There must be a lot of Sunday newspaper readers who feel as I do at the moment.

Memo to self: You blew it.

Monday 2 February

I suppose the first surprise was that Arnold Thacker didn't remember any of us. It was stupid of us to imagine that he would. If he has had more than thirty boys in his class every year for thirty years, he's had a thousand pupils suffering from his demented spite and none of them for more than twelve months. But we have only had to remember half-a-dozen teachers who came into our lives when a young memory retains such things and carries them around for years.

He hadn't changed a lot. Even at 28, or however old he was when he taught us, he was a shrivelled little bastard with piercing eyes and protruding ears. The years had obviously felt that no further depredations were necessary.

We all shook his hand and ushered him into the dining-room we had used before. Luke, who organized this migration, was wearing a shiny green suit which was presumably the product of his recent shopping splurge. It looked hideous. We sat down and looked at one another uncomfortably. Waiters came and went.

'So this is what happened to the boys of the sixties,' said Thacker. 'It's very interesting to see you all. I'd like to thank you for inviting me. It's most kind.'

'What's your life like now, Mr Thacker?' Jamie asked. 'Now that you've hung up your cane?'

'The days are empty.' Thacker said, ignoring or not hearing Jamie's little joke.

'And how's the school?'

Thacker's reply to this was delayed by the arrival of the food. Tonight we were all on lamb which had been specially recommended, except for Paul Ross who was still on spaghetti. Half-a-dozen bottles of red wine appeared along with one bottle of Evian water.

'The school?' said Thacker, as Luke filled our wine glasses. 'It's not a grammar school any more. It's something they call a sixth form college. They've turned the education system on its head.'

'And is the end product any more successful?' asked Andrew Burrows who was paying more attention to the wine than the food. He had also been drinking in the bar before we arrived.

'More successful than what?' Thacker asked.

'The bunch of failures you produced here.' Thacker looked at him and seemed at a loss for a reply, so Andrew ploughed on with a line he had obviously prepared. 'Let's face it, Arnold, you were to teaching what Long John Silver was to tap dancing. What persuaded you to take it up?'

'I had the best qualifications of my year.'

I wasn't going to let Andrew Burrows monopolize this exchange. My limited fund of charm had been exhausted by the handshake. 'But you couldn't actually teach, could you?' I said. 'You couldn't transfer knowledge into pupils' heads. You certainly left none in mine.'

Thacker, who was making a spirited assault on the wine, took this with quiet aplomb. 'Some pupils' heads were impenetrable,' he said with a little laugh.

'Who was your most successful pupil?' Luke asked.

'From your era? Unquestionably Nicholas Beresford Waynflete. He was a brilliant lad.'

'He was a prat,' said Paul Ross. 'Why did he have three names when the rest of us had two?'

'Inferiority complex,' I said. 'Like Iain Duncan Smith.'

'It wasn't a complex; he was inferior,' Paul Ross said. 'Do you know where he is now, Mr Thacker?'

'Thriving in the City is my guess.'

'He's in prison. A thirty-seven million pound bank fraud.'

Thacker looked sad. 'Good lord. Well, he was a good boy when I taught him.'

'Even that isn't true,' I said. 'He was the shop-lifting champion of his year.'

'He specialized in what the Australians call the five finger discount,' said Luke. 'He could get you anything. He even brought back the right size in jeans.'

'I hear the tinkle of shattered illusions,' said Andrew Burrows.

Thacker looked at him. 'I don't remember you.'

'You'd remember my backside: you caned it often enough.'

Thacker emptied his glass and refilled it. I thought he was

taking it rather well, but he had spent his working life facing a hostile audience.

'You boys seem to have a bit of a gripe about the old school,' he said amiably.

'Some schools boast that they produce confidence without arrogance,' I said. 'Others manage to produce arrogance without confidence. Ours did neither.'

Thacker drank more wine and looked at me over the top of the glass. 'Our intention,' he explained when he had lowered his drink, 'was to produce young men who were upright, honest and hard-working.'

'But hard-working at what?' Luke asked. 'Stacking supermarket shelves? Where was the ambition? Where was the dream?'

When the waiter arrived to take orders for dessert, Thacker opted for cheese and celery, a choice, I thought, that permitted further drinking. He was quaffing the stuff as if red wine was a fond memory from a more prosperous past.

'Why do you boys regard yourselves as failures, anyway?' he asked as he attacked his Camembert.

Luke gave him the roll call. 'Paul, who wanted to be a vet, is a traffic warden. Andrew, who aimed to be a millionaire, is a bankrupt. Jamie lives in a shed on forty quid a week. I have no job, and Mark runs a small bookshop.'

'A mouse in the rat race of life,' I said.

'You told me I'd got the brains of a rocking horse,' said Jamie. 'Hardly encourages a chap to stand for Parliament, does it?'

'You'd be over-qualified, I'd have thought,' I said.

'You were obsessed with discipline and punishment,' Jamie told him. 'It didn't seem to cross your mind that these kids would have to go out into a competitive world and earn a living. There was no praise or encouragement. No attempt to instil confidence.'

'If our aim was to crush you it doesn't seem to have worked,' Thacker said mildly. 'What I see round this table are five lively gentlemen.'

'Luckily our education didn't stop on the day we left school,' Luke said. 'School tried to teach us that we were worthless, but we later discovered otherwise.'

The depth of the animosity around this table was only now dawning on Arnold Thacker who had misguidedly thought that some of the earlier remarks were all part of the drunken banter of a men's night out. He was beginning to look uneasy.

'Luke asked where the dream was. You knocked it out of us with your cane,' said Paul Ross.

This was one remark too many. Thacker stood up slowly. 'You'll have to excuse me,' he said. 'I need some air.' He made his way rather unsteadily to the door by the windows which led out into the gardens.

'Do you think we've been too hard on him?' Paul Ross asked when Thacker had disappeared into the night.

'Hard on him?' said Andrew. 'I was just warming up.'

'Go and fetch the sod,' said Jamie. 'I was just getting into my stride.' But he regaled us instead with stories of his life among the upper classes, the money and the marijuana, the aristocratic adulteresses, titled nymphomaniacs and insatiable heiresses. It was half an hour before our attention returned to Thacker's absence.

'I'd better go and look for him,' I said. 'He's probably asleep under a tree.'

'I'll come with you as I invited him,' said Luke, and we went out into the dark. I took one side of the grounds and Luke took the other. I was looking for a drunken heap huddled beneath a tree but found nothing. It occurred to me that Thacker might have made his way round to the front and driven off in his car, but I pressed on to the far end of the grounds where a twenty-foot high yew hedge protected the hotel's privacy. I poked around there, wondered whether Thacker had sought sanctuary among its dark green narrow leaves, when I suddenly heard Luke shout, 'Found him!'

I hurried in the direction of his voice. 'Is he all right?' I asked, as I approached. Luke looked ashen.

'Not exactly,' he said. 'He's face down in the lake.'

Luke, who wasn't about to ruin his new suit, stared at the floating ex-teacher as if there had been some mistake. I rushed to where his body lay in the water and had to wade in for two or three yards before I could reach his feet. I pulled him out and laid him on the grass.

'It may not be too late,' I said. 'Where's the pulse?'

'He's dead,' said Luke. 'I can tell you that now. I've seen a couple on Sydney beach. The clue is his eyes are open.'

'What about the kiss of life?'

'Pass,' said Luke.

The rest of the evening was a nightmare. Luke hurried off to find the manager who phoned the police and ambulance service. I returned to our dining-room where the conversation had moved on with the help of the wine to the religious beliefs of Paul Ross. (Jamie wanted to know why Mars wasn't mentioned in the Bible.)

'Where's Thacker?' he asked, when I went in.

'He's dead.'

'How do you mean – dead?'

'Dead, as in deceased. He drowned in the lake.' An appalled silence greeted this news. I sat down and looked at my wet feet. 'Not a very pretty end to the evening.'

'Do you mean he fell in?' Jamie asked.

'How do I know? He was face down in the water.'

Paul Ross's expression had assumed a pious glow. 'Nemesis,

the goddess of retribution, has paid us a visit tonight,' he declared solemnly.

Within minutes a police car had pulled up at the back of the hotel, followed soon afterwards by an ambulance. I got up and watched from the window. There were flashes from a police camera and then the area where Thacker entered the water was cordoned off with police tapes.

The hotel manager, a big red-faced man who looked as if he spent too much time in his own bar, stuck his head in the door and called to Luke, 'Mr Dyson, the police would like your guests to stay until they can have a word with them.'

'That's it,' said Andrew, hauling himself wearily to his feet. 'I'm off to the bar.' The alcohol had given him a curious conversational tic. Jamie had become the broken-down beatnik, I was the bibulous bookman, and Luke was the alcoholic Australian. But he surpassed himself when he asked the policeman who had come to interview us what he had done with the 'waterlogged pedagogue'.

'Sober up, Andrew,' said Luke, who still looked sick from his discovery.

'It's been a bacchanalian evening, officer,' Andrew explained to the bemused detective. I watched his performance with fascination. Sober, he verged on the inarticulate. 'We want to help you crack this case,' he said reassuringly. 'With our brains and your cunning we'll disentangle the conundrum in no time.' He belched sonorously.

The policeman gave him a dismissive look and turned to us. 'It looks like an accident or suicide and not a crime,' he said. 'Of course, suicide used to be a crime.'

'What did you do – take the defendants to court in a hearse?' Andrew asked.

The policeman stared at him. 'I don't think you can help us any more, sir. You can go home now.' Had he known that

Andrew was driving, he might have thought twice about this suggestion. He looked at the rest of us. 'The man who drowned,' he said. 'What can you tell me about him?'

I stood there with my feet squelching in my shoes while Luke produced the information the policeman wanted. I decided to go home as soon as possible but there was one more delay as the detective insisted on recording the names and addresses of us all.

The ideal evening doesn't end with your name and address in a policeman's notebook.

Memo to self: The next time Luke says he's had an idea feign deafness.

Tuesday 3 February

Driving home drunk last night Andrew Burrows had the bright idea of overtaking a Lamborghini when a BMW was approaching in the other lane. The subsequent three-car collision miraculously produced no fatalities, although the BMW driver was taken to hospital with concussion. Andrew emerged unscathed aside from bruises, but his Ford was destroyed. He is acquiring an old Honda tomorrow for further adventures on the highway.

We learned this when we returned tonight to the Walton Hall hotel. A series of phone calls from Luke had suggested that we should all meet for a post-mortem on the events of last night which had ended somewhat inconclusively – I was keen to get away to dry my feet, Andrew was too drunk to make sense, and Luke was still in a state of shock.

Tonight we sat soberly in the bar and sipped lager guiltily like defectors from a Rechabite rally. Paul Ross, drinking Pellegrino, watched our restraint approvingly, but Andrew, with a marvellous multi-coloured bruise on his forehead, still managed to drink faster than any of us. I looked at him and wondered whether there was a connection between his heavy drinking and his tortured sexuality: was he drowning his sorrows in buckets of hooch or just a greedy pig?

'I've made some enquiries,' said Luke, as if calling a meeting to order. 'Arnold Thacker was a widower whose wife died some years ago. There were no children.'

'What's the significance of that?' asked Andrew.

'Well, I thought it made yesterday's events easier to bear. On the other hand it complicates the question of his funeral. Who will organize it? How will we know when it is?'

'Do we want to know?' asked Jamie.

'I think we ought to go.'

'What the hell for?'

'It'll look good.'

'To whom?'

'The police. I thought they looked bloody suspicious yesterday. As if we were in some way responsible.'

'Which we certainly were,' said Paul Ross. 'I had nightmares last night.' He grimaced at the memory of them.

'What we don't want is an inquest verdict of suicide,' I said. 'We want the coroner to decide it was an accident. If it's suicide people will start to ask why he did it.'

Jamie asked Luke, 'How did you find out that Thacker was a widower?'

'I rang the headmaster at the school. Some new bloke called Young. He was Thacker's boss in the last few years he was a teacher. He had to suspend him once for beating a boy. Apparently you're not allowed to do that any more.'

'What about the police?' I asked. 'Have you seen them today?'

'They were snooping around for a while, brandishing tape

measures. I kept out of their way, but my friend Bernie spoke to them.'

'Who's Bernie?'

'The manager. They told him that an autopsy would reveal whether Thacker had been assaulted. They'll also find out how much he had drunk.'

'That should clarify matters,' I said.

The next subject was whether in this strangely abstemious atmosphere a second pint of lager was allowed. Luke resolved the matter by buying a round. After all, Andrew was on his fourth.

And then came the highlight of the evening. At exactly ten o'clock Marilyn Monroe walked in. Shirley Burrows, extensively and voluptuously reconstructed in an approximate image of the lamented star, glided seductively across the floor in a knee-length white dress. The slim and shapely figure, with huge breasts and a pretty face surrounded by a mass of carefully arranged blonde hair, reduced most of our group to a dumbfounded but grateful silence. Only Luke retained the power of speech.

'Jesus Christ!' he said admiringly. 'If that was my wife I don't think I'd be considering homosexuality.'

When she reached us he leapt to his feet and kissed her on the cheek. The rest of us were placed inconveniently round the table for such intimacy.

'You used to kiss me on the mouth, Luke Dyson,' she said.

'But you were Shirley Appleton then,' said Luke. 'No husband.'

She looked at us all and smiled. 'The class of … when was it?'

'Don't ask,' I said.

'You're wearing well.'

'Not as well as you, Shirley,' said Luke, who seemed to be infatuated with her seductive image. 'Why are you here?'

She indicated her husband whom she had so far ignored. 'Didn't that lunk tell you? He wrote off his car last night so I have to drive him home.'

Luke, who now obviously regarded last night's disastrous crash as a fortuitous pile-up, was reduced to stupid grins and whimpering noises, so I asked Shirley, 'Can I get you a drink?'

She waved the car keys at me. 'I think one of us better hang on to a driving licence.'

Andrew, now absolved from this responsibility, was heading for the bar again, so Luke put his arm round Shirley and said, 'Marry me, Shirley. What your life needs is a good man.'

'You're right there, Luke,' she said. 'Do you know where I can find one?'

Memo to self: Now I can visit Marisa.

Wednesday 4 February

Invading the salon of culture where Marisa reigned was a daunting prospect, but it wasn't the brilliant craftsmanship and surrounding aesthetic achievements that intimidated me: it was the unknown reception I was going to receive.

On the crowded pavement of Brewer Street a girl in an unseasonal mini-skirt was selling flowers and I paused to consider buying some. I decided that if my welcome was chilly, flowers would only add to the embarrassment, and I walked on until Picture This was beside me and could not be avoided. Attempting to exhibit a demeanour that somehow combined nonchalance and panache, I stepped inside.

Marisa, in a blue silky trouser suit today, was adjusting a picture that hung on the furthest wall, and she turned as she heard the door. I walked forward in silence, not knowing whether she had recognized me. When we were six feet apart I stopped and smiled, but it was Marisa who spoke.

'What kept you?'

I laughed at the wit of it. 'That remark deserves an Oscar.'

'I've had a long time to rehearse it.'

'You look fantastic, Marisa,' I said, and meant it.

'You don't look so bad yourself. Can I make you a coffee?'

She disappeared through a door at the back of the gallery and I looked round at the paintings. The Japanese polka dot fetishist had been replaced by the works of a seventeenth-century Danish artist, described as an enigmatic illusionist, whose most celebrated accomplishment was a painting showing the back of a painting so that it looked as if it had been hung back to front on the wall.

'It's what we call *trompe l'oeil*,' said Marisa, returning with coffees. She put them on a small table at the back of the gallery and sat on one of two chairs that were pulled up to it. She waved me towards the other.

'So,' she said when I had sat down, 'why are you here?'

'Because I've only recently found out where you were. You disappeared off my radar.'

She looked quite lovely sitting there, and watching me with her cool blue eyes. 'Perhaps your radar didn't work from Canada,' she suggested.

'You don't know how much I regret that trip,' I told her. 'Particularly when I got home to find that you'd vanished.'

She played with a pen on the table. Printed up one side it said PICTURE THIS. 'You should have married me before you left,' she said. 'I was ready.'

'I was seventeen. I had no job and no money. How could I get married?'

'You were a big boy. You got a summa cum laude in the haystack.'

I didn't allow the compliment to deflect me. 'Of course if I'd known that you were going to end up with a morose, teetotal vegetarian with a religious problem I'd have acted differently. Why did you marry him?'

'You know what they say. If you want the rainbow you've got to put up with the rain.'

'In this context, it's difficult to see what the rainbow is.'

Marisa turned her head as if her answer required some thought. 'Companionship, money,' she replied eventually. 'He was a kind man until he became a bit odd. The religion thing followed the job loss. I suppose it's where people go in a crisis. The Cabinet minister who went to prison and then came out to announce that he was going to study theology. It's bizarre. People need props.'

'They do. I use a liquid they make in Scotland.'

'And are you married?'

'I seem to be.' She responded with a little grimace that was difficult to read. Her lovely black hair had been cut short which gave her a sporty look. 'And now we're both in the culture dispensing business,' I said, hurrying away from the idea that I should have a wife. 'The demand is not huge.'

'In my case it doesn't matter,' Marisa said. 'This gallery is owned by a certain titled gentleman who appears in the gossip columns more often than he does in here. He pays me handsomely to run it. It's the prestige, you see. I don't think he knows Picasso from Paganini, but people think he does and that's what counts in this world, isn't it?'

'The public perception.'

'Exactly. Anyway, he's due in here this morning for our monthly meeting so you may catch a glimpse of him.'

'I hope not,' I said. 'It's you I've come to see.'

'And I'm glad you did, but it never occurred to me that I'd have to wait until the third millennium to see you again.'

When she got up to clear the coffee cups away in preparation for her boss's arrival, I had a sense of opportunities being lost. I had signed up Mrs Pringle for the day and was prepared for a long and possibly painful conversation which would bring us eventually to the delicate subject of Marisa's son.

But it was not to be.

'He's here,' said Marisa, after removing the cups. 'Pretend you're an art critic. Look intelligent.'

I turned and saw an old man coming through the door at the other end of the gallery.

'You'll have to go, I'm afraid,' said Marisa.

His lordship, a short plump man of about seventy, was making his way towards us despite various physical ailments which obviously hampered his progress. One leg worked better than the other, and his breathing wasn't coming from an athlete. I recognized him from Press pictures and remembered when I saw him that the appellation 'Soho art gallery owner' was usually attached to any mention of his illustrious name. He had a huge nose that sprouted a profusion of grey hairs and unruly hair higher up that hung over his ears. Despite his inferior appearance he ignored me.

His untimely arrival comprehensively balked any hope I had of further conversation.

'I'll phone you,' said Marisa.

Memo to self: But will she?

Friday 6 February

I had decided that Paul Ross was several annas short of a rupee but now he has gone completely potty. Talking to a friend who is a reporter on the *Gazette* he wondered aloud whether our treatment of Arnold Thacker had persuaded him to kill himself. So today's paper carries the two-line banner headline:

DID EX-PUPILS DRIVE
TEACHER TO SUICIDE?

Fortunately the only name mentioned in the story is Paul Ross himself who is quoted as saying, 'I must admit we weren't very kind to him. As a Christian I naturally had misgivings about this, but there was a feeling round the table that there were scores to be settled.'

The story says that Thacker left the table 'in a distraught state' after suffering abuse from men he had taught more than thirty years earlier.

'"I can't pretend that Mr Thacker was the most pleasant teacher we had, but it's a long time to harbour a grudge," said Mr Ross, 49.'

The most ominous part of the story was the first sentence: 'Police are investigating a theory that a 60-year-old former teacher was driven to suicide by the taunts of his former pupils.'

Police? Are men with handcuffs about to disturb the placid ambience of my shop? Am I on the run?

I tried to ring Paul Ross to convey a few home truths but peripatetic traffic wardens are difficult to reach and so I phoned Luke at the hotel. He rang off while he went off to find a copy of the *Gazette*.

'Jesus Christ!' he said when he called back. 'Is Paul Ross mad?'

'That was my conclusion,' I told him.

'Is there any charge the police over here could dredge up if they thought it was true?'

'There's no charge the police can't dredge up if they want to put someone in court, although I can't think what it would be. They could get you for being rude to your neighbour if they wanted to – behaviour likely to cause a breach of the peace, or something like that.'

'In France they'd call it involuntary homicide,' said Luke. 'Causing a death without intending to.'

'What we call manslaughter.'

'Hang on,' said Luke. 'This is getting silly. They can't arrest people because they were the last person a suicide spoke to. "Did you say something that depressed him? You're nicked!"'

'It wasn't suicide anyway,' I said. 'He's not the type. He was drunk and tripped into the lake.'

'You're sure of that, are you?'

'Pretty sure. But that doesn't mean that the police couldn't harass us for a few days until they discover it for themselves.'

Half an hour later I found the truth of this. A police sergeant came into the shop and asked for me. I took him to the back, not wanting to alarm what few customers I had.

'We're curious, Mr Hutton, about what transpired between you and your friends and Arnold Thacker before his body was found in the lake,' he said, withdrawing a fat blue notebook from his pocket.

'Yes, I've read the newspaper,' I said. 'Paul Ross is talking drivel, which isn't unusual. Thacker was our guest and we were probably too generous with the red wine. He went outside to clear his head.'

The sergeant looked at me. 'And what's the answer to my question?'

'We had a go at him, certainly. He was an appalling teacher who beat boys regularly. We felt obliged to point out some of his shortcomings.'

'And how did he take it?'

'He wasn't happy. But I've never seen him happy.'

'He was described as being distraught.'

'By whom?'

'The paper said that.'

'It's in the papers, it must be true?'

I'd scored a small point and for a moment the police sergeant faltered before gathering his thoughts. 'I'm trying to discover what frame of mind Mr Thacker was in when he left the hotel,' he said.

'He was drunk,' I replied. 'He'd had more alcohol than he should have done.'

'And what do you think happened then?'

'He wandered out into the hotel grounds that he wasn't familiar with. It was dark and he stumbled into the lake. He was too drunk to save himself.'

'Well forensic will be telling us something about that. There was no physical involvement?'

'Do you mean did we hit him? We weren't even with him. For God's sake, we're talking about a drunk man of sixty.'

'Forensic will be telling us about that, as well.'

'I suggest you wait for their report then.'

When he had gone I tried another phone call to Paul Ross's mobile: this time he answered.

'What the hell are you doing, Paul?' I asked. 'Have you seen the paper?'

'Yes, I'm sorry about that,' he said. 'It was a mistake.'

'It certainly was.'

'He's my next-door neighbour. I was chatting to him. I didn't realize he was going to put it in the paper.'

'But you knew he was a journalist?'

'Oh yes. I knew he was a reporter on the *Gazette*.'

'That's what journalists do, Paul. They print stories in newspapers. See you in prison.'

I hung up before he could reply. You would think that an

idealistic twerp who doesn't live in the real world couldn't do a lot of harm, but Paul Ross might yet prove this theory wrong.

Monday 9 February

Snow.

Tuesday 10 February

More snow. Four inches deep now.

Wednesday 18 February

Marisa hasn't rung. I'm surprised and depressed. Two whole weeks have elapsed since I visited the gallery and now I've started to wonder what could explain the silence. Has she had second thoughts? Is she playing a game?

I'm naturally tempted to ring her, but I feel a call from me might put too much pressure on her. I've made the approach and must let her decide how to react to it.

Thursday 19 February

After a grisly fortnight of examinations, probes and forensic tests, the police finally released the body of Arnold Thacker and he was cremated today. Luke insisted on attending this melancholy event and persuaded me to accompany him. Jamie Croft, with a life whose emptiness can only be imagined, cycled to the hotel and accompanied Luke in the Porsche. I think he just wanted something to do.

What the police discovered will presumably remain a mystery until the inquest. There were no uniformed gentlemen at the funeral to ask.

Only one other couple were there. If you don't have any friends in life, you're certainly not going to acquire them in death. The couple turned out to be Thacker's brother and his wife. They had dutifully come down from Yorkshire, but didn't appear too dejected by Arnold's departure. Apparently they hadn't even met for six years.

Afterwards Luke, Jamie and I returned to the hotel where a small drama awaited us. We were sitting at the bar with halves of lager and trying to shake off our funereal mood, when an expression invaded Luke's face which combined shock, alarm and disbelief. It had obviously been caused by a new arrival in the bar because he was looking over my shoulder at the door. I thought the only appearance that could create this effect at this moment was Arnold Thacker's, but when I looked round I saw a rather good-looking blonde striding purposefully towards us.

'Christ almighty!' Luke whispered. 'It's my wife.'

Nicole Dyson was dressed casual-smart, a short-sleeved white linen jacket and beige trousers – the clothes somebody might wear on a long-distance flight.

'Well, hallo,' said Luke, who was totally thrown by this intrusion. 'How long have you been here?'

'I landed an hour ago and got a taxi,' said Nicole in a genuine Australian accent – 'I lended' rather than 'landed'. She looked remarkably spry for somebody who had just spent a day sitting on a plane. 'I've some business in London to attend to, and there's an exhibition I want to see. So I thought I'd drop in here first to make sure you were still alive.'

'Nicole has a thriving interior design business,' Luke explained, and then embarked on some belated introductions.

'I half remember you,' she said to me. 'I enjoy the letters you send Luke.'

'This is the man they called the prince of the beatniks,' Luke said. 'You've read a few things about him in the papers.'

'Indeed I have,' said Nicole. 'Jamie Croft! Are you still chasing rich women?'

'They're becoming harder to find,' said Jamie.

'Really? I wouldn't have thought you'd have any trouble.' And she gave him a smile that seemed to carry more weight than the usual polite greeting.

Luke noticed this and hurried the conversation on. 'Where are you going, Nicole?' he asked.

'I've a hotel booked in London, and a taxi waiting outside. But we've got to meet for a talk while I'm here. It's my birthday next month.'

'I know that. Are you looking for a present?'

'Yes, a divorce.'

Luke didn't look as surprised by this as I thought he would. Perhaps he was still thinking about Shirley Burrows. 'If that's what you want, kid,' he said calmly. 'But let's keep the lawyers out of it. I don't need a ventriloquist.'

Nicole was a different woman today to the girl Luke had picked up in a coffee bar thirty-odd years ago. Success in the interior design business had given her a confidence, even a brusqueness, that was quite threatening. I guess that laid-back Luke found her difficult to handle, but then women sometimes were hard to deal with. You couldn't ignore them or hit them as you would a man. The challenge didn't go away.

'My life needs a makeover,' Nicole said now. 'It's time to move on.'

I stood up, faintly embarrassed to be sitting in on this. 'It's time for me to move on,' I said. 'I've got to relieve Mrs Pringle in the shop. Nicole, interesting to meet you again.' I slipped out, leaving them to rake over what were evidently the dying embers of their marriage: it wasn't a spectator sport.

Two hours later Luke rang me at the shop.

'Something rather odd has happened,' he said.

'Yes, I watched it,' I told him. 'Your wife doesn't mince words, does she?'

'No, not that. Jamie's bike is still propped up at the front of the hotel.'

'A bit of a blemish against that elegant façade.'

'You don't get it, do you? He obviously left in Nicole's taxi.'

'That was kind of her,' I said.

'It depends where she's taking him.'

'Oh, got you.'

'She fancied him. I spotted it immediately. He'll be shagging her senseless in the Waldorf Astoria by now.'

'I don't think it's called that any more. There've been mergers and acquisitions in your absence. Anyway, he told me that he was embarrassed to do it with anyone over the age of twenty-five.'

'Nicole will help him to overcome that little phobia. I saw the look in her eye.'

'Why does she want a divorce, anyway? Did she say?'

'Yes, she said that she got fed up with me being at home all day. Apparently husbands are supposed to disappear after breakfast, and not reappear until the evening. But I just sat around like a cabbage.'

'A cabbage?'

'That's what she said.'

'I thought she'd overlooked your green and wrinkly appearance.'

'It's no joke, Mark. My marriage is disintegrating around me here.'

'You didn't seem too upset when she said she wanted a divorce. She's a very confident lady, isn't she?'

'She's a very successful lady. That's the trouble. She earns three times what I earn, and is a bit of legend in Brisbane with her bloody interior designs. People are told that what they need is the bloody Nicole Dyson touch. When we met she looked up to me, then she looked straight at me, and now she looks down at me.'

'That's the story of marriage,' I said.

'Still, I dreamed about Shirley Burrows last night. I fell out of bed twice.'

'And she wasn't even there! What's your next move?'

'First thing tomorrow I'm going to drive to Jamie's shed. If he's there I can bring him back to collect his bike. If he's not, it means he's moved in with Nicole.'

A customer was waving a book at me that he wanted to pay for. It was David Beckham's latest autobiography.

'Let me know what happens,' I said. I hung up and headed for the money. I don't suppose Nicole Dyson in her quest for riches wastes her time on whimsical telephone conversations.

Memo to self: A pay-off at last for the prince of the beatniks?

Friday 20 February

The local paper hasn't lost its capacity to deliver a Friday morning shock. Today the *Gazette* informs me that my wife's fat friend Phoebe has actually sold the novel she was telling me about on New Year's Eve. It's going to be published! It's going to end up on my shelves! I read the story in disbelief.

> Local nursery teacher Phoebe Davenport has sold her first novel to one of Britain's biggest publishers. It will be out in the autumn.

'They were the first publisher to see it and they took it straight away,' said a delighted Miss Davenport, who is 31. 'They think there might be a film in it.'

The original title was *The Lonely Road* but the publishers have persuaded her to change it to *How to Bin Your Husband*.

'Basically it's a look at the sheer impossibility of men and women living together in peace,' said Miss Davenport. 'Their interests are too diverse.'

She was reluctant at first to change the title, but the publishers have convinced her that the new one is more arresting and will sell more copies.

The story went on for half a column, telling us about Phoebe's career as a teacher, and her sudden decision to write a novel. Apparently she has never written anything before.

I had only just put the paper down when she came into the shop. She was wearing a blue towelling track suit which made her seem rounder than ever.

'Have you seen the paper?' she asked.

'I have. Congratulations.'

'It's wonderful, isn't it? What happens now?'

'How do you mean?'

'How do I get the book into shops like this one?'

'Oh well,' I told her, 'your publishers will do that. A salesman with dandruff will no doubt turn up here and try to persuade me to take more copies than I can possibly sell.'

'How many will you take?'

'Six is the usual number, but I reckon in your case we'll sell four dozen. Have you got a lot of friends who will be buying it?'

'Loads.'

I could imagine who they were. I regarded her as one of the devious female mafiosi who saw as their primary function the protection of women's unthreatened rights.

'We're in business then,' I said.

She laughed delightedly, and then suddenly looked serious. 'I had two reasons for coming in. The second was to ask about Emma. Where is she? You haven't put her out in a wheelie bin, have you?'

'We don't all have your imagination, Phoebe,' I said. 'She's staying with her parents in the Isle of Man where she's appearing in a film and fulfilling her acting ambitions.'

'That's wonderful,' she said.

'No, it's not. I can't cook.'

'My God, you sound like a scene from my novel.'

'Perhaps if they film it you can get Emma a part?'

'That would be marvellous, wouldn't it? Can you give me her address?'

I went back to my desk to write out the address of my in-laws. Everybody's life seemed to be moving faster than mine. The women, with their dramatic career changes, were leaving me for dead, and even Luke, who had never seemed like a star, had dumped a stash away in a London bank before flying nonchalantly round the world.

'I'd like to hear what she says,' I told Phoebe, as I gave her the address. But there was no satisfaction here either.

'I can't promise that, Mark,' she said. 'It might be confidential.'

Memo to self: I was right. The rewards are going to the wrong people.

Saturday 21 February

When Luke woke up yesterday morning Jamie's Croft's yellow bike was still leaning incongruously against the immaculate front of the Walton Hall Hotel. Without a second thought, he climbed into the Porsche and booted it to Jamie's shed. Getting no response there, he headed for London. The hotel where Nicole was staying in the Aldwych seemed to have ten times more staff than Walton Hall, most of them bilingual. One of them told him, after a quick phone call, that Mrs Dyson would see him in her room.

I heard all about it this morning when Luke arrived in the shop looking glum. This was quite different to the large smile that Nicole had been wearing when she admitted him to her luxurious bedroom. She was wearing clothes that he had never seen before, a smart two-piece in deep brown, brightened by gold threads.

'I'm glad you've come,' she said. 'There are things we have to discuss.'

'What have you been up to?' he asked.

'I'm going to have the best holiday of my life. Theatres, concerts, films, shops, restaurants. I think I'll be staying for two or three weeks.'

Then Luke saw a familiar pair of beige suede boots beside the large double bed.

'You've got Jamie here,' he said.

'How clever of you, darling,' said Nicole.

'I suppose it was a blow to my pride,' Luke said to me in the shop. 'I asked her why he was there, and she said she needed an escort in London, someone who knew where everything was. I mentioned that taxi drivers were quite good at that sort of thing and she said there was no need to get nasty. I said, "What's he done then, gone out in his socks?" She said she'd bought him some shoes among other things.'

'Jamie's still looking for a rich woman then,' I said.

'He's found one,' said Luke. 'She even paid me back the two hundred quid I'd lent him. I warned her not to take responsibility for his debts as they could be quite extensive. She said,

"Don't worry about me. Men I can handle". I told her that Jamie was a professional philanderer, and she said what more could a woman need at her age? It was too late for an amateur.'

'She fancies him obviously, and you can see why,' I suggested. 'He spent years pleasing women. He's had more experience with intelligent women than any other twenty men you can think of. He knows when to be kind and considerate. He understands the little things that matter. He's never boring.'

Luke reluctantly accepted some of this. 'It's been his job. He knows all about it like you know about books.'

'Will she take him back to Australia?' I asked.

'Oh, I don't think so. This is a holiday affair. She gets good company and an escort to the theatre, and he gets money and decent food.'

Then he told me what was said when she took him downstairs to one of the hotel's restaurants for coffee.

'What we want is a clean break,' Nicole had announced, 'so that we can both walk away owing nothing. It should be easy to arrange. We're both civilized people.'

'None of the normal acrimonious haggling, you mean?'

'Exactly.'

'You're taking all the fun out of divorce, Nicole,' he told her.

But she was wearing her businesswoman's hat. 'Here's my offer,' she said. 'We have two assets. One is my business which I naturally want to hang on to. The other is the house.'

'Which you also want to hang on to.'

'I do, actually. So I'm going to buy it off you. That way I don't end up with everything.'

Luke, seeing a substantial jackpot coming his way, nodded.

'The thing is,' his wife told him, 'you are a shareholder in the design business, so I think that in renouncing all your rights there you should be paid full price for the house. What do you think?'

'I think it's very fair,' said Luke. 'Any idea what it's worth?'

'As a matter of fact I have. I had it valued before I flew over.'

'You think of everything.'

'I try to, darling. One of us has to. The agent said three hundred thousand dollars.'

Luke, apparently, was pleasantly surprised by this figure and tried to see it in pounds sterling. 'I don't know what the exchange rate is at the moment,' he said. 'Events have put me out of touch.'

'I've checked that,' said the businesswoman. 'You'd get about a hundred and thirty thousand. But you've got to come over to Oz to sign a few documents in the presence of a lawyer. The divorce is pretty straightforward if there's no dispute, and we can deal with that at the same time.'

'Go back and organize it, and I'll follow you over,' he said. 'By the way, where is Jamie?'

'He's gone out to buy some theatre tickets for tonight. *Krapp's Last Tape*, or *Tape's Last Crap*. I don't know much about Samuel Beckett.'

'So there you have it,' said Luke in the shop. 'The end of a marriage.'

'Conducted with icy efficiency,' I said. 'You're lucky. My wife doesn't even communicate.'

'Does she want a divorce?'

'She hasn't told me what she wants. What about you? What are your plans for the future?'

Luke's face shed the mask of depression that had accompanied his sad London narrative and suddenly assumed an artful glow. 'Have you heard of Shirley Burrows?'

'Would that be the girl formerly known as Shirley Appleton and now a dead ringer for Marilyn Monroe?'

'That's her.'

'What about her?'

'I want to do things to her that haven't been invented yet.'

Memo to self: Phoebe's right. Marriage is dead.

Tuesday 24 February

The brisk efficiency with which the Dysons have handled their marital break-up has left me feeling inadequate. I sit here, waiting to be swamped by the crazed fans of Kazuo Ishiguro, wondering what the future plans for me. Marisa hasn't phoned. I struggle to compose a new verse but some days your brain doesn't work that way.

I am reduced to doing a crossword. Orifice – eight letters. A glance at the other clues reveals that it starts with an A and ends with E but I can't believe that even a newspaper as shoddy as this one would include arsehole in its crossword answers.

Thoughts of Emma the absent wife begin to invade my thoughts after listening to Luke's story, and suddenly, on a whim, I get up and go next door to the travel agents from which I return with a brochure that features the Isle of Man. I could fly there from Gatwick for only £99 so long as it was at a weekend.

I hadn't realized that there was much to say about the Isle of Man, but the brochure had thought of things. Two hundred square miles of beautiful countryside and a wonderful coastline of beaches and coves! The oldest parliament in the world – and the world's largest waterwheel! Horse-drawn trams and a mountain railway that takes you to the summit of Snaefell!

But why would I go? It was unlikely that I would receive a warm reception. If Emma wanted to talk to me she could come here or pick up a phone. But I want to escape from the limbo in which I now languish. I want the matter resolved.

I put the brochure in my drawer and decided to think about it.

I returned to the crossword. Orifice – eight letters. Aperture, obviously.

MARCH

Every year back Spring comes, with nasty little
birds yapping their fool heads off, and the
ground all mucked up with arbutus.
– *Dorothy Parker*

Monday 1 March

Today was a day to remember, but that owed nothing to the first person to visit the shop, a brash young man with salesman written all over him. The sales reps drop in like bees on honey and, as I don't belong to one of the big chains, I have to deal with them. The selection of books here is not imposed from above.

Today's visitor, who was waiting outside with a bag of books when I arrived, turned out to be not only a salesman but also an author and a publisher – he was marketing his own books.

'I've been on a sexual tour of the world which I'm turning into a series of paperbacks,' he said proudly. He plunged into his bag and came up with three of them. I saw the title *Bonking In Bangkok* on one, and *Legover in Lanzarote* on another.

'Punchy titles,' I said, 'but not for us.' He looked crest-fallen. The paperbacks were smart and he had obviously put time, money and effort into this potential earner. 'The outlet you want is the corner newsagent. You'll catch the passing trade.'

'I want to get them into proper bookshops as well,' he said.

'The ladies who come in here looking for Dick Francis or P.D. James would probably faint if they were confronted by' – I pointed at the third book – '*Handjobs in Honolulu*.'

He put the books back in his bag, but left me his card.

When he had gone I retired to my desk for the first coffee of the morning. As usual, I wondered whether I had made the right decision. If the public's taste, shaped by newspapers and warped by television, was going down perhaps I should go down with it before I was left stranded on the high ground with unsold copies of Dostoevski and Jean-Paul Sartre.

I drank my coffee and stared at the pad on my desk. Another dud verse fell effortlessly from my pen.

She was a card, that girl
In her heart she wanted diamonds
But she fell for a gardener with his spade
And now she's in the club.

I was reading this and worrying over the third line when the phone rang.

'It's only me,' said Marisa.

'*Only*? This is the most important call I've had this year.'

'Well I promised to ring you. I'm sorry it's taken so long. There have been one or two unsettling moments at home.'

'What?' I asked.

'Do you think Paul could be homosexual? I mean, could it happen at his age?'

'I never put anything past anybody,' I said. 'That way I get fewer shocks.'

'He seems to be developing some sort of rapport with Andrew Burrows.'

'And how does this rapport manifest itself?'

'Phone calls mostly. Long interminable phone calls. Of course, I've no way of knowing what goes on when I'm at work. Still, that's not why I rang. It was lovely seeing you the other day.'

'Would you like to see me again? I'm so available it's humiliating.'

'Where's your wife in all this?'

'She's not in all this. She's living with her parents in the Isle of Man.'

'In that case what about dinner one evening?'

'Just say where and I'll bring money.'

'Not in town,' said Marisa. 'I like to get out of London when I'm not working. How about some discreet up-market joint in the country?'

'I know the very place,' I said.

Memo to self: Yippee!

Wedneday 3 March

As I had weakly promised to deliver them, I took Charles Westacott's books round to his house this evening and he invited me in for a drink while he wrote the cheque.

'I'm sorry it's taken so long,' I said. 'One of them was being reprinted.'

'And did they give you the picture?'

'Yes. You're going to the House of Lords. Congratulations. I've never met a lord before.'

The drink that he provided was sloe gin which I rather enjoyed.

'I've got to think of a place for the title,' he said. 'Lord Westacott of – where? I was born in Kelstern in Lincolnshire. Lord Westacott of Kelstern. What do you think?'

'It sounds good,' I said.

Janet, hearing voices, came in. She had just returned from a visit to her reflexologist, and was now making gin and tonic jelly. Gin seemed to be in vogue in the Westacott home this evening.

'Lady Westacott,' I said. 'What a privilege to share your company!'

'We're not quite there yet,' said Charles. 'But I've resigned my seat. What a relief that was. No more having to listen to tendentious crap from my idiot agent. We had a glorious row at our last meeting. My motto is, if you haven't got anything nice to say about somebody, say something nasty, and my agent, I'm afraid, was unglued. He didn't have both oars in the water.'

'That man made my teeth itch,' Janet said vehemently.

'He always spoke very well of you,' her husband told her, winking at me.

'I can barely contain my indifference,' she replied, taking a sloe gin from Charles. 'How are you, Mark? Surviving on your own?'

'Just about.'

'Have you heard from Emma?'

'Oddly enough, no.'

'Oh, we have. We got a lovely letter.'

I wasn't surprised. She always attached a curious importance to her friendship with them. I suppose it was the money. She obviously hasn't bothered to write to her friend Phoebe, an oversight she will regret when she hears about the novel.

'What did she say?' I asked. I was fairly confident that she wouldn't discuss her marriage in a letter to Janet – it would be demeaning.

'She's in a film. Isn't that wonderful? It's called *The Devil's Spouse*, and Rupert's directing it. He has a lovely visual sense apparently.'

'What part is she playing?' I asked.

'Oh, not a major role. It's her first film. But she's got quite a lot of lines and they're all raving about her. Isn't she a clever girl?'

I was being prompted for an endorsement here. Janet was

digging with no great subtlety to see how things were between us.

I stonewalled it. 'She's unique,' I said, 'like everybody else.'

When I left, Charles escorted me to the door and handed me the cheque.

'Good luck,' I said, 'among the toffs.'

'All the world's a stage, and I've been assigned a new role,' he said with mock modesty. He had quit his constituency in a flurry of valedictory abuse and was now going on confidently to higher things. How easy some people find it to convince themselves that they're important.

Memo to self: If all the world's a stage, where is the audience sitting?

Wednesday 10 March

I was staying in this evening, reading *The Bookseller*, studying publishers' catalogues and doing what I regard as my homework, when the door-bell rang. Unexpected callers in Trebor Avenue are too often charity collectors, political candidates grovelling for support, or one of those sanctimonious religionists, convinced in their madness that they know something I don't. Their gall always offends me. But it was a little late for that type of visitor and curiosity drove me to the door.

Standing on the step in a smart brown suit was Jamie Croft. I couldn't have been more surprised if it had been the President of the United States.

'How did you know where I live?' I asked.

'You're in the phone book.'

'And how did you get here?'

'Taxi. Look, I've come to buy you a drink. I can hardly look up Luke. Any good pubs around here?'

'A new suit, a taxi, buying drinks! Did you win the Lottery?'

'In a way,' he said.

I took him to the Perkin Warbeck, a pub I occasionally used when tedium threatened to overwhelm me. It was a comfortable well-furnished place where the level of conversation quite frequently rose above football and television. It also sold my favourite lager.

Jamie produced a new suede wallet from the inside pocket of his jacket and it seemed to be stuffed with folding money. We collected our drinks and retired to a table in a corner which had leather-backed seats and fresh beer-mats.

'Did you hear what happened?' Jamie asked.

'Yes, you've been bonking Mrs Dyson.'

'And you disapprove?'

'I don't pass moral judgements on my friends, Jamie,' I told him. 'What's going to happen?'

He looked despondent. 'Nothing. She flew back to Australia this afternoon.'

'A holiday fling? Still, there seem to have been some benefits,' I said, feeling the lapel of his jacket.

'She's making a lot of money. I don't think even Luke realizes how much.'

'You keep finding these rich women and losing them, Jamie.'

He shrugged. 'I'm a bit deficient in the image department these days. A bloke on a bike who lives in a shed? I'm hardly likely to disappear into the sunset with a princess on my arm, am I?'

'How much did she give you?'

'Ah, the direct question. You should have been a journalist, Mark. She gave me two thousand quid in a plastic envelope and told me to buy some clothes. Then she bought me a pair of Evisu jeans adorned with rhinestones that cost a grand.'

'All dressed up and nowhere to go.'

'You said it. Still, I can always flog the stuff. What do I need a suit for? I only wore it tonight to give you a surprise.'

When I got up to buy him a drink he looked a lonely figure sitting at the table. He was missing Nicole. I bought two lagers. A sign behind the bar said FREE BEER TOMORROW but I suppose you have to expect a sense of humour in a pub that has been named after a Flemish impostor.

'In the days when you were the scourge of the upper classes, you'd have found a new woman by now,' I said, as I handed him the drink.

He smiled, flattered by the remark. 'Those were the days. Making love to Ravel's *Bolero* in a chalet in the Swiss Alps with a whiff of pot in the air.'

'Words like rat and drainpipe spring to mind.'

He drank some of the lager. 'I'll tell you something: the girls are getting prettier today. Twenty-five years ago a quarter of them looked like dogs, but now there are stunners all over the place.'

'Oh good. You're still noticing. That's encouraging.'

'But they don't notice me. Nicole should never have flown off. We got on really well.'

When I stood outside with him waiting for the taxi he seemed a pathetic figure. The spirit had gone out of him. He had seen the promised land and experienced a tantalizing glimpse of the possible and now it had been taken away. I felt more sorry for him than I had when I first saw him lying on a mattress on the floor of his shed.

Friday 12 March

I don't know where to begin. It was certainly an evening I shall never forget. We met in the small cocktail bar at the front of a fifteenth-century coaching inn that had been converted in the prosperous eighties into an elegant restaurant. I had already ordered a bottle of Veuve Clicquot which cost me £40 before she arrived in a little red Golf. She was wearing a smart green suit which stopped at the knees. I kissed her – but on the cheek.

A waiter poured the champagne and we sat at the little oak bar while we waited for someone to bring menus.

'I love living in the countryside,' she said. 'I saw a crested crane on the way to work this morning.'

'How do you know it was on its way to work?'

She made what the French call a *moue*. 'I'd forgotten about your awful sense of humour.' She looked round. 'This is a lovely place, isn't it?'

'A lovely place for a lovely lady. Listen, I have a question for you. What are you doing for the rest of your life?'

The question startled her. 'Oh golly. I don't know.'

'Having a gay husband isn't going to be fun.'

'It's not fun now. It's as if he's got a new head.'

A waiter appeared with two large menus. Marisa wanted melon followed by roast duck, and I was too preoccupied to read menus and ordered the same. When we were summoned into the restaurant we were given a pleasant table by a window that afforded spectacular views of the Sussex countryside.

'So what are we going to do about it?' I asked, before the conversation could drift off in another direction.

'We?' said Marisa. 'Is there a "we"?'

'In my dreams.'

The melon arrived at that moment and I ordered wine. Marisa wanted white and I wanted red, so I asked for an expensive white wine and a cheap red one.

'These dreams,' said Marisa. 'Do I figure in them?'

'Figure in them? You dominate them.'

'That's lovely to hear, Mark. I hope I behave myself.'

'Not always, I'm glad to say.'

A new expression on her face brought back vivid memories of the uninhibited girl in the haystack, but her words soon hauled me back to the present. 'If you're saying what I think you're saying we've got to have a serious talk first,' she said, meeting my loving gaze with a look that pre-empted trivia.

'I don't do serious talks,' I told her. 'They spoil dinner. I want you, Marisa. I always have.'

She gave me a look which insofar as I could interpret it suggested that I should get a grip on myself. 'There are things you need to know.'

'What do you mean? You haven't been voting Conservative, have you?'

She finished her melon and looked out of the window. A flock of swallows, back early from their African watering grounds, swooped over the Downs snatching insects from the air. 'I'll tell you my story when the duck arrives,' she said. 'It won't stand interruptions from the waiter.'

'I like stories,' I said. 'Is it a good one?'

But Marisa was looking serious again. 'I did something I've been ashamed of ever since. I carry the guilt round with me and it'll be a relief to talk to you.'

'My God, you *did* vote Conservative!' I refilled her glass and saw that she was not amused.

The waiter arrived to remove plates and another, hovering behind him, immediately delivered the roast duck. The restaurant, commended in all the best food guides, was nearly full, and all the customers looked elderly, prosperous and well fed.

'The moment you went to Canada I had Paul on the phone,' Marisa said, starting on her duck.

'Is this the story?'

'This is the story. He wasn't so bad in those days, in case you've forgotten. He was young, hopeful and ambitious. What he wanted was a date.'

'He always fancied you,' I said, remembering his boasting about becoming a vet.

'Anyway, in those days if you didn't have a date you didn't go out. So I went out with him a couple of times, once to a cinema and once to somebody's party. There were a lot of parties in those days. There was always somebody throwing one on a Saturday night. The kids don't seem to do that any more. I suppose I was a bit annoyed with you for pushing off to Canada and leaving me on my own. I was young. I had a life to lead. The third time he asked me out, to a concert at the Festival Hall, he asked me to marry him. I turned him down, of course. I was waiting for you. But I have to say, if it doesn't sound too conceited, he was totally obsessed with me. The next time we met, with other people at a dance, he went down on one knee and asked me to marry him. When I turned him down, he said that he would go on asking until I accepted. It got to be a bit of a joke. Well, you can guess what happened next. I discovered I was pregnant – by you, not him. I panicked. My parents were not the type to want a daughter around the house who was an unmarried mother. It was bad news in those days, and awkward with the neighbours.'

'It was different then,' I said. 'Today they look surprised if you *do* get married.'

'That's progress. Anyway, the next time he asked me I said yes. The baby was born three weeks late which helped people believe it was Paul's, and he has believed it to this day. Are you shocked?'

'I knew all this, Marisa.'

'You knew?'

'At the first of Luke's dinners Paul showed me a photograph which left me in no doubt. That three generation shot of Paul, Mark and Mark's baby son. I took one look at Mark and knew. It was why I decided to come and see you.'

'My God, it must have been awful for you.'

'It was a bit of a bombshell to discover that you were a father and a grandfather on the same evening when you thought that you had never had any children.'

Marisa looked miserably at her wine. 'I end up hurting everybody. More guilt.'

'How was Paul hurt exactly? He doesn't even know.'

'He had to give up his ambition to be a vet, because he couldn't afford to study for six years or whatever it was. He had a wife and a baby to support and he was still in his teens. He had to find a job. It changed his life. And then I insisted on calling the baby Mark which hurt him a bit. But he put money and love into that child.'

I fell silent at the picture she had evoked. I had heard often enough about the effort and sacrifice involved in parenting, but I had made neither effort nor sacrifices myself.

'So,' said Marisa, 'what do you think of me now?'

I looked at her lovely face and saw an expression of pure concern. 'I'm sorry for you,' I said. 'I'm sorry for me. I'm sorry for all of us. Can I ask you a question?'

'I think a question is the least that you're entitled to.'

'About my son.'

'Well there the news is good, I'm happy to say. As Paul felt that his own education had been cut short, he put a lot of effort into Mark's. He sent him to public school, and urged him to keep studying. He was still a pupil when he was twenty-six!'

'And now?'

'He's a doctor.'

This came as quite a shock. I was accustomed to young men

becoming salesmen or civil servants or soldiers. But young Mark had not had his confidence undermined by Thacker's dubious tuition.

'Where?'

'Not far away. He works in a hospital near Banstead. He's a psychiatrist.'

'Good God,' I said. 'I wonder where he got his brains from?'

'My father, who adores him, says from him. He says these things often skip a generation.'

'How is your father, by the way?' I felt obliged to ask. As the father of a psychiatrist I had more important things to discuss.

Marisa said her parents were both alive and well. Her father had retired after a rewarding life in the City, and taken his money to Dorset where they lived in a mansion near Dorchester. Having lost both my parents several years ago to two different lethal diseases, I envied her this continuation of family life. There had been many occasions when I would have liked to sit down and talk with my mother and father. I shook off the familiar regret by drinking more wine.

'My son,' I said.

'Mark Junior.'

'I assume he knows nothing about all this?'

Marisa drank some wine herself. 'I thought of telling him many times. I felt he ought to know. But then I wondered whether it would unsettle him. And then there was the question of Paul. How could I tell one without the other finding out? In the end I didn't have the nerve. Should I have done?'

'Probably not, but I think he ought to know now.'

'Are you going to tell him?'

'Am I going to meet him?'

'We ought to arrange something.'

'Would I like him?'

'Oh, you'll like him. He's a charmer.'

'Like his dad?'

'Oh Mark,' she said, 'what are we going to do?'

Our plates were empty and the service was prompt. I wasn't sure whether this was due to the restaurant's vaunted efficiency, or because the table was booked for a later sitting by customers who were already quaffing sherbet in the cocktail bar and hungrily studying menus. Marisa wanted trifle so I ordered it too.

'Do you always copy your partner, or do you sometimes make your own decisions?' Marisa asked, but I was more interested in her previous question.

'You ask what we are going to do. We're going to do what we should have done all those years ago – get married.'

'So far as I can recall,' said Marisa with a wry smile, 'we're both married already.'

'I was thirty-two,' I told her. 'I waited fourteen years for you but you'd disappeared. I didn't even know you were married until two months ago today. Paul broke it to me over dinner. "Marisa sends her love", he said. "Marisa Wynn?" I asked eagerly. "No, Marisa Ross", he said. I couldn't believe what I was hearing.'

Marisa met my eyes but said nothing for a moment. 'Well I've explained how it happened,' she said eventually. 'If you hadn't been in Canada ...'

'The biggest mistake of my life,' I admitted, 'but let's look to the future.'

'What do you see?'

'Initial problems, subsequent bliss.'

'God, I hope you're right. What's your wife doing in the Isle of Man, anyway? It seems an unlikely destination for anyone.'

The trifle arrived at that moment and I demolished it with relish. The meals I had been cooking for myself, dragged from a tin or grabbed from an uninviting supermarket shelf, gave tonight's feast a magical quality.

'My wife is a film star,' I said. 'My son is a psychiatrist and my wife is a film star. I've only discovered this in the last few days. It's bloody humbling, actually.'

I told Marisa about Rupert, the extremely famous film director I'd never heard of, and how a mysterious relationship had been forged between him and my wife. 'And now she's appearing in some movie he's making called *The Devil's Spouse* which they're filming in the Isle of Man.'

Marisa took this sensational information without a change of expression. 'What's humbling?' she asked.

'Look at what these people are achieving and then consider what I've done – stand in a shop and flog books.'

'My God,' said Marisa, 'I'm dealing with a tormented soul.'

'When I decided I wanted to be self-employed and bought the bookshop I thought I'd chosen the brave option. It now looks like the weak-headed one. No triumphs, no brief shining moments. I'm a failure, Marisa. Will you marry me?'

'As soon as possible please.'

Saturday 13 March

So what do I do? Lying awake in bed this morning, half listening to the shrill interruptions of the lady on the 'Today' programme who had plenty of questions but couldn't bear to wait for the answers, I decided that I had to talk to Emma. People today don't bother to get married until they have two or three kids, but some long-ago promise made me want Marisa to be my wife.

One of the thoughts that has haunted me recently has suddenly assumed a new relevance: I don't have a pension. I considered it from time to time but pension schemes were getting bad publicity in the wake of the recession and it looked as if the money that would one day arrive would be less than the figure originally promised. It's not too late for me to join one now, but my age would no doubt mean that the final pay-out would be a lot less than younger and more far-sighted folk would be receiving.

Perhaps if Emma and I are divorced she'll have to give me some of her movie loot: in these days of sex equality alimony is two-way traffic.

I decided to write to her. She was going to be difficult to reach on the phone, and telephone conversations get misquoted or partially forgotten.

Emma dear, I wrote when I'd opened the shop, *your abrupt departure and subsequent silence leave me in a quandary. I expect that your cruel wit will prompt you to say that there's nothing new about that, but I am left with certain problems that need to be resolved. Can you tell me what your intentions are? The thing is, I want to get married but, as you probably remember, I am married to you. Congratulations on your movie debut. I was pretty impressed as you can imagine. How did it all come about? And who's Rupert? I'm ready to fly to the Isle of Man if there's any chance of a discussion, but I don't know how busy you are.*

This seemed a rather short letter, but after two months of silence I thought that anything more would cast me in the role of humble supplicant.

Thursday 18 March

Back comes a reply from the Isle of Man. It starts 'Dear Hutton' because Hutton is what Emma always calls me. She has hardly used my first name since I've known her.

Dear Hutton,

I've only been gone ten weeks and you're thinking of getting married again? You move quickly, don't you? And I always likened you to a terrapin on Prozac! Are you sure that somebody you have known for such a short time is the right person? I think I should save you from yourself and refuse to divorce you.

I'm sorry about my abrupt departure as you call it. It was difficult to explain to you because you were unconscious. Basically, I was offered the chance of a lifetime so long as I was available immediately. Filming is a strange and slow business but I'm getting used to it.

Don't come to the Isle of Man. I hardly have time to sleep. Shooting finishes here in June although there will be some studio scenes to be filmed afterwards, probably at Pinewood. I'll be back for the Westacott garden party in July and we'll talk then.

Byeee!

I read the letter a couple of times, put it down, and then read it again. It was what was missing that interested me. She had ignored my invitation to discuss Rupert; she had failed to answer my question about her intentions; and she left open the question of where she would stay when she turned up for the summer party that the Westacotts were apparently holding.

I secretly hoped that long before July Marisa would have sorted out the problems attached to her deviant husband and moved in with me.

Memo to self: Two women in the same house? I can't imagine it.

Saturday 20 March

Luke limped into the shop this morning like a man who has been kicked repeatedly in the testicles by a sixteen-stone rugby player.

'I've been seduced,' he said. He abandoned the exaggerated gait, but even when he tried to walk normally it didn't look right. He seemed grateful to reach the chair at the back of the shop and slumped into it.

'What do you mean, seduced?' I asked.

'A woman made sexual demands on my body.'

'Some visually impaired tart, was it?'

'Shirley Burrows – or Shirley Appleton, as I still think of her.'

'I'd better make you a coffee while you tell me about it.'

'After thirty quiet years among the sheep and kangaroos, I'm beginning to wonder whether England holds more excitement than I can handle,' he said. 'I've so far been clobbered with a divorce demand, seduced by a sexual prodigy and confronted by a corpse in a lake.'

'So how did you and Shirley team up?' I asked, when I'd made coffee.

'I bumped into her in town and suggested a drink. Well, one thing led to another and the next thing I knew I was spreadeagled on her carpet with my trousers round my ankles.'

I sat down, trying not to imagine this. 'It's not safe for a chap to go out alone these days. You need to carry one of those whistles.'

He nodded as if this deserved serious consideration.

'We went back to her house for something to eat as neither of us had anything to do. She knew Andrew was round at Paul's. Suddenly she pulled a bow on her shoulder and her little blue dress, which was all she was wearing, fell to the floor. It was as if the Queen had unveiled a statue, without the usual hitches. So there she was, Marilyn Monroe in the nude. Mark, she's got the practised skills of a veteran hooker. Something extraordinary in her musculature, or perhaps a trick she learned, enables her to delay your orgasm while prolonging her own. I tell you, after twenty minutes I didn't know whether I was going to ejaculate or die. The threat of a cardiac arrest was the least of my worries. I was more concerned about whether I would ever get my sexual organs back and, if so, what condition they'd be in. It was like being raked by a combine harvester.'

'It sounds awful.'

'It was bloody wonderful. Apparently her last boyfriend, an ex-wrestler with biceps like steel, is in a wheelchair, but she doesn't think there's any connection.'

I wasn't so sure. After Luke's account of his demolition on the carpet I could see big and powerful men reduced to a pitiful state of debauched decrepitude by a joust with the reconstructed charms of Mrs Burrows. When they'd regained sufficient strength to stand up they would probably mull over the compensations of celibacy.

'What am I going to do?' he asked.

'Castration is probably the best option, but you'd have to go private. The National Health Service doesn't do it.'

Luke ignored this and looked serious. 'I've got to be good enough for her,' he said. 'I must admit that after the first occasion I wondered whether my health was robust enough to survive another date. It took me three days to walk properly and I still seem to sit down a lot. But I've got the solution in my own hands, haven't I? The hotel's got a gym. A morning jog round the Sussex lanes, a couple of hours in the gym, a protein diet and the odd press-up by an open window should turn me into the sex machine the situation demands.'

'I've heard of people training for the London Marathon, but they usually raise money for charity.'

'Sponsor me,' he suggested. 'A fiver a jump.' He was fired with enthusiasm now for a training regime that would lift him to some illusory height of sexual achievement. 'Punishing your body in preparation for a bonk that will make your teeth rattle seems an intelligent use of my time. She'll probably kill me with her intricate talents but there's every chance that a worse death is waiting for me down the road.'

I removed his empty coffee cup and glanced at the shop: three customers happily reading but no sign that they wanted to pay for the pleasure.

'I hear Nicole's flown off,' I said, to change the subject.

'How did you know that?'

'I saw Jamie.'

'I bet he's depressed. I think he thought he was on a winner.'

'He was depressed. You're right. Are you off to Australia to tie up the loose ends?'

This reminder brought a smile to his tired face. 'And I'll come back a rich and free man! But I can't go over until after the Thacker inquest. I've got to give evidence apparently.'

'Why's that?'

'I'm the bloke who discovered the body, aren't I?'

'I hope nobody is going to talk about taunting pupils.'

'I'm dreading it to be honest. I'm going to concentrate my thoughts on Shirley. Much more cheerful.' He hauled himself to his feet. It was a big effort.

'Where are you going?' I asked.

'To the gym.'

Memo to self: There are no gains without pains. – Adlai Stevenson.

Monday 22 March

I rang Marisa and suggested lunch, having bribed Mrs Pringle with a copy of the new Jackie Collins. Marisa said she could only get out for an hour because she wasn't supposed to shut the gallery during the day.

We hurried through the street towards food, blocked occasionally by tourists studying the *A to Z*, and waiters examining the racing pages on their way to a betting shop.

'Do long-haired youngsters still play guitars in coffee bars in Soho?' I asked nostalgically.

'Sadly they grew up and left,' Marisa said. 'The businesses round here are strange now. There's a chap across the road who will give you an Indian head massage. Lots of tapping.'

She led me into a pleasant Italian restaurant where the tables were large and the lights were low. Waiters in green and white aprons buzzed around like confused flies.

I gave her my news. 'I've finally heard from my wife,' I told her when we sat down. I handed her the letter.

A small waiter with a black moustache took our order. As Marisa wanted lasagne, I ordered cannelloni so that I could not be accused of copying her. The customers in this restaurant were television people or advertising executives or men who had their own little film companies tucked away in second-floor studios where they made commercials for dog food or soup. Nobody here, I thought, would waste their lives in a struggling bookshop.

'Bad news,' said Marisa, returning the letter. 'She doesn't seem to commit herself to anything.'

'Well,' I said, worried by her tone, 'I think we can safely say that my marriage is over.'

'That's not clear from the letter, is it? What had you told her?'

'That I want to remarry.'

'Which she's going to block. And what happens when she comes back to this party in July? I certainly don't want to be living in your house when she turns up.'

I could understand this but hated to hear it. The food arrived as I considered what I could do. A girl, a model I had seen on magazine covers, came in wearing a blue catsuit. Her escort was a face from one of the new boy bands. They were shown to a privileged corner where he placed a proprietary paw in her lap.

I turned my attention back to Marisa. She was prettier than ever in a pink blouse and black wrap-around skirt, but Emma's letter had dimmed the brightness in her eyes. She put her hand on mine and said, 'I was hoping I'd be living with you soon, but I think we'll have to put that idea on hold. I thought your wife was living in the Isle of Man. I didn't realize she could reappear.'

There was a reproach here, a hint that I had somehow misled her, and I felt sick.

'You will be living with me soon,' I promised. 'I'm going to sort the Emma business out. It's difficult to nail at the moment when she's in the Isle of Man and doesn't answer any of my questions.'

'I think she intends to stay married to you,' Marisa said. 'It's her house too.'

'How is it with Paul?' I asked. 'Have you talked to him?'

'As far as I can see Andrew Burrows spends most of his time in our house when I'm not there.'

'How do you know that?'

'Empty beer cans, chocolate wrappers, toilet seats left up. Paul only works three days a week and obviously spends the rest of his time entertaining his boyfriend. I find it all very depressing.'

'I'm going to rescue you from that depression.'

She smiled at last. 'I wish you would.'

APRIL

Oh, to be in England,
Now that April's there.
– *Robert Browning*

Thursday 1 April

It's my fiftieth birthday today. Mrs Pringle, who knows all about traumatic milestones having reached the advanced age of sixty-one, insisted that I take the day off and I readily agreed. She probably imagines that I am out carousing somewhere but I find nothing to celebrate. I sometimes wonder whether being born on April Fool's Day was an ominous augury about what was to come.

I have spent the day holed up in Hutton Towers or, to be precise, the three-bedroom semi-detached in Trebor Avenue where I have lived since my marriage. I sat in the kitchen with a coffee and tried to review the detritus of my life, and how things have changed while I've been trying to live it.

When I was born the Prime Minister was Winston Churchill which sounds like the dark ages now. I remember the assassination of President Kennedy when I was ten, and England winning the World Cup when I was thirteen. My father celebrated with bottles of John Courage. It was the first beer I ever drank.

I remember it all vividly. It's last week that's a bit muzzy. And the world has changed so much it's hard to keep up.

Apparently we send twice as many e-mails as posted letters. We use computers to develop holiday snaps. We've got picture messaging, wireless internet, broadband jukeboxes, 3G phones and MP3 players, smaller than a pen, that hold your entire music collection.

The rules have changed. A smoking ban is spreading. You buy drinking water in bottles instead of getting it from a tap. You can swear on television. Pubs are open all day, but teenage girls aren't safe on their own in the street. Drivers must wear belts. Nobody smokes pipes.

The language has changed. People say 'up to speed' instead of 'up to date', 'state of the art' instead of 'latest', 'get off my case' instead of 'leave me alone', 'lost the plot' instead of 'confused', 'hidden agenda' instead of 'secret motive', 'I've got a problem with it' instead of 'I don't like it', 'I can see where you're coming from' instead of 'I know what you mean' and dozens of other strange words and phrases like 'down-shifting', 'cutting edge', 'take on board' and 'up for it'.

The second bedroom upstairs is kept for guests although there have been few of them. The third bedroom has become a kind of junk room and this afternoon I went in and turned it upside down in a search for relics from my past. I found a hoard.

School reports ('Mark has brains but seems reluctant to use them' – Arnold Thacker), photograph albums (Mark, aged three, on a tricycle with his parents watching), love letter received at the age of ten ('Dear Mark, will you be my sweatheart?'), several long-forgotten toys and, best of all, some old diaries which kept me entertained for a couple of hours this afternoon.

I was about sixteen when I received a page-a-day diary among my Christmas presents. The following year I meticulously filled it in and the habit has obviously stuck. Settled comfortably on the sofa I read some of those entries from the past with a mixture of mirth and mystification.

March 6

Dick Clark claims to have fondled Gwyneth's breasts but we don't believe him. She doesn't look as if she has had her breasts fondled and if she wanted them fondled she would hardly ask Dick Clark.

April 12

We had cadets all morning. Brown and Tubb fainted.

April 26

I'm going to be a playwright and have written my first play. We performed it after school in the gym and it got a lot of laughs. It is set in a dentist's and written like Shakespeare. The lines that got the biggest laughs were:

If you have teeth prepare to shed them now.

I want the tooth, the whole tooth and nothing but the tooth.

I come to take your teeth out, not to fill them. The good food that you bite you swallow, the bad is oft embedded in your teeth.

June 20

Walking round town I didn't wear my school cap which is contrary to the laws of the school as laid down in 1832. An inquisitive prefect asked me why my head was bare and I explained to him that my cap was two sizes too small and I had as yet failed to convince the pater that the expenditure the acquisition of a new one would incur is either necessary or worthwhile. This excuse did not go down too well with the result that I had to write a 750-word essay for this prefect which I entitled 'Essay for a Worm'. He said: 'I'm thinking of giving you another essay for insolence.' I said it was a good job he was only thinking about it.

July 12

We have started to issue our weekly ratings. My latest ones are:

1. Judy Tiernan
2. Muriel Woodger
3. Beryl Heard
4. Maureen Higgins
5. Rosemary Loveland
6. Jane Plumridge

July 28

Jumbo Knight masturbated into his pants during geography and showed us the semen on his hands to prove it. People were pretty impressed because nobody else had done it. Jumbo has got a new name now. He's called Tosser.

Reading this stuff was not just a journey into the recent past,; it was like visiting another age. The narrator was unknown to me. I don't remember writing a play or an 'Essay for a Worm'. And who was the stroppy pupil who got away with cheeking prefects? L.P. Hartley was right: the past is a foreign country.

I dragged myself away from this unproductive diversion and packed all the mementoes from another era into the suitcase in which I found them. Would I ever see them again?

I went downstairs and pulled a can of Stella Artois from the fridge. It was my birthday. I deserved a drink.

Memo to self: Why didn't I get a single birthday card? And why aren't girls called Rosemary any more?

Friday 9 April

Sitting in the coroner's court this morning and waiting to hear the consequences of our uncharitable treatment of Arnold Thacker was rather like sitting in one of his classes and waiting to hear the inevitable punishment for some trivial breach of the rules.

I sat in the front row with Luke. Behind us Paul Ross and Andrew Burrows sat together like two bugs in a rug. It was too far for Jamie to cycle, and Luke, evidently, was not inclined to pick him up.

Three court officials and two policemen – assigned non-speaking roles in this mini-drama – stood up suddenly and we saw the coroner approach his raised desk from a door at the back of the courtroom. He was a serious, grey-haired man with a thin, pale face which suggested that digging out the facts on death was not the jolliest option in the jobs market. In front of him, at a much lower desk, a clerk sat with pen poised.

The detective sergeant who had questioned us all on the night of the death was the first to give evidence. He told the coroner how he had been summoned to the hotel by the manager who led him to a body by the side of the lake. The body, he said, was subsequently identified as that of a retired teacher called Arnold Thacker.

Luke was called next. He told the coroner how Thacker had left his dinner party to get some fresh air, and when he didn't return Luke had gone out to look for him and found him face down in the hotel's lake.

'Had he been drinking?' the coroner asked, and when Luke said there had been a few glasses of red wine some judicial notes were made on the coroner's pad.

The third witness was a Mrs Hannah Mitchell who had been staying at the hotel and had seen Thacker walking into the lake. The coroner asked her about Thacker's gait as he approached the water. Was he moving quickly or slowly? Was he stumbling? Did he appear to be drunk? Mrs Mitchell gave a theatrical performance which seemed to combine slowness, stumbling and drunkenness, but lacked speed.

The coroner listened to most of this evidence with his eyes shut, but whether this was because he was trying to imagine the scene, or merely fatigue, we were not to know.

The fourth and, as it turned out, final witness was the doctor who conducted a post-mortem. He stepped smartly into the witness box in a dark-grey suit, white shirt and rather fetching pale-blue tie. He almost looked too young to be a doctor, but he sounded like Tony Blair.

His revelation that the cause of death was drowning was hardly a surprise, but he went on to reveal the excessive amount of alcohol in the deceased's body, although, he felt it necessary to report, there were no drugs.

I was waiting for somebody to bring up the subject of taunting pupils, but this was looking increasingly like a groundless fear. However there was still the possibility of a suicide verdict which would open up the subject if people started to wonder why Thacker had decided to terminate his life in this way.

Suddenly the coroner was addressing the room in a gentle northern accent, and he went straight to the heart of my worries.

He said that a suicide verdict was a serious matter. It had legal consequences for the bereaved family, and was always difficult to prove in the absence of a suicide note. It was not a verdict he would bring in lightly, and he wasn't disposed to bring it in now. Two verdicts were available after the evidence they had heard. One was an open verdict, which meant that the cause of Thacker's death remained uncertain. The other was misadventure which referred to an accidental death not due to crime or negligence.

The coroner gathered up his papers; his departure was imminent.

'Who knows what happened in the grounds of the Walton

Hall Hotel that evening?' he asked. 'Mrs Mitchell saw Mr Thacker walk into the water, but she could hardly interpret his intentions at that distance. He could have been walking drunkenly in the dusk, not seeing where he was going. The doctor has testified to the amount of alcohol in the body, and it was more than enough to get him banned had he been driving a car. The confused state of his mind is now something that we can only guess at. I propose to record a verdict of misadventure.'

While the clerk sitting in front of him made frantic notes, the coroner stood up and nipped smartly through the door at the back as if in some discreet bar nearby his drink was already poured. He left a relieved silence behind him.

'Thank God for that,' said Luke as we stood up.

Outside I approached Paul Ross.

'I had the police round thanks to your little effort with your journalist friend,' I told him. 'It was all rather unnecessary, wasn't it?'

His response took me by surprise. 'How's my wife?' he asked, pushing his face towards me in a sad attempt to appear threatening.

'Pretty fed up, I should think, given the company she keeps.'

The reply incensed him. 'And you're going to comfort her, are you?' he shouted.

Andrew Burrows put a restraining hand on his shoulder. 'Leave it, Paul. Let's go. It doesn't matter.' It was odd to see Andrew sober. He carried the authority he had once presumably enjoyed in his fluctuating career before it lurched from prosperity to bankruptcy. They walked off together towards the car-park.

'What was that all about?' Luke asked. 'Are you seeing Marisa?'

'I'm trying to,' I said.

Thursday 15 April

A lifeline! Mrs Pringle, my tenant, my assistant, and my favourite person this morning, came down from her flat clutching a copy of the *Daily Mail*.

'There's something in here that will interest you,' she said.

I took the paper from her and flicked through the pages: homicidal housewives … cancer cures … anger over asylum seekers … more pictures of the Beckhams.

'Give me a clue,' I said.

'The gossip column.'

I turned to the gossip page and there it was: A STAR IS BORN (AT 38). This somewhat ungallant headline appeared over a photograph of my wife kissing a man with a passion that had been rarely exhibited in Trebor Avenue.

My gaze switched with mixed feelings to the caption that ran below.

> Rupert Barkley, director of the hit movie *The Donkey Tree*, has another success on his hands – and another woman on his arm.
>
> Barkley, 45, is shooting his new film *The Devil's Spouse* in the Isle of Man where he was caught (above) canoodling with his new star, Emma Benson.
>
> The twice-married director chose Emma, 38, for his movie despite the fact that she has never appeared in a film before.
>
> Insiders say that her performance is remarkable and predict great things for her and the film.

'So she's not Emma Hutton any more,' said Mrs Pringle disapprovingly.

'It doesn't look like it,' I said. 'Perhaps Benson is a better name for a film star.'

'It looks as if she's going to be Emma Barkley in a minute.'

'I do hope so,' I said.

When Mrs Pringle left, I rang Marisa at the gallery.

'The *Daily Mail*, page 35,' I said.

'I've got one here. Hang on.' I heard the sound of rustled newsprint. 'What am I supposed to be looking at?'

'That woman snogging in the picture. That's my wife.'

'Is it, by God! She's rather pretty, isn't she?'

'Never mind pretty,' I said. 'This is good news. Don't you see?'

There was a pause while she read the caption. 'There's hope for us after all, isn't there?' she said when she'd read it.

'There certainly is,' I assured her. 'Things are going to move.'

Memo to self: Show me a straw and I'll clutch it.

Tuesday 27 April

Luke is off to Australia to try to retrieve the remnants of his life from the overpaid and no doubt intransigent lawyers who have been hired to protect Nicole's interests. The plan is that he will return reborn – with his freedom, his money and such dusty relics from his past that he can find, pack and dispatch to England, probably by boat.

It was necessary, apparently, for this epoch-making odyssey to be marked by a dinner at the hotel. I went gladly – the warmed-up meals I was grabbing from supermarket shelves were leaving holes in my diet and similarly vacant spaces in my stomach.

The punishing rigour of the gym, on the other hand, had

given Luke an athlete's sheen. He bounced into the bar on the balls of his feet as if a fifteen-round world championship fight was something he could now accommodate.

'You're talking to a shagging machine,' he said proudly. 'Shirley's pretty impressed.'

'Are you allowed to drink lager, or do you have to have fruit juice?' I asked.

'Bookworms like you could do with some exercise.'

'Shagging machines like you would benefit from a good book.'

'I read a book with no pictures once,' he said. 'What a long month that was.'

Over dinner his thoughts turned to Australia and Nicole. There was no doubt he had been hurt by the peremptory way in which he had been dumped, and was now apprehensive about what problems were waiting for him in Australia.

'She's unpredictable,' he said. 'One day we were coasting along quite happily, and the next she was demanding a trial separation. That's Sheilas for you. Still, you've had the same thing yourself.'

'Not really,' I had to admit. 'Emma's dissatisfaction and frustration had been apparent for some time. She wanted to spread her wings, and I wasn't giving her what she wanted, financially, socially or probably sexually. It's difficult to make love to a woman when she's been slagging you off for two hours.'

This dismal dissection of two turbulent affairs each heading for their own rancorous denouement seemed profitless, and I asked Luke what his plans were when he returned to England.

'I'm booking out of the hotel before I go so I won't have anywhere to live. I'm handing back the hire car so I won't have wheels. Do you think Jamie's got any spare room in his shed?'

I should have offered him a room in Trebor Avenue at this

point, but I was clinging to the hope that Marisa would move in soon, and another guest would spoil the fun.

'What about Shirley?' I asked.

'I live in hope. It's a bit difficult at the moment with Andrew stumbling drunkenly around the premises.'

Drinking the wine – a classic Rioja, I'm glad to say, and not one of Luke's Australian selections – I was struck by the similarity of our positions. We were both trying to extricate ourselves from a marriage that had failed. Both marriages had been pronounced dead by the wife. In each case, despite the rebuff, we had our eyes on a new partner, and both of these new and fanciable ladies had seen their husbands reject them for the company of men.

Memo to self: Life is obviously a game of two halves.

MAY

The sun is set, the spring is gone
We frolic while 'tis May.
– *Thomas Gray*

Sunday 2 May

I turned on the television this evening, and before I could switch to Ceefax or Teletext which is where I normally reside – not wanting to watch somebody paint a wall or dig a garden – I was confronted by a familiar face that I couldn't identify. I ransacked my unreliable memory searching for clues. The only certain fact that floated to the surface was that this was someone I had met, and not some modern 'celebrity' who had grinned at me from a hoarding. I tried to place the face in the correct surroundings and decided that I had met him in the shop.

The sound was turned down as usual. When I turned it up I recognized the voice, but that still didn't help. He was talking rather knowledgeably about sex, and I listened, fascinated.

And then the truth hit me, and gave me a nasty shock. This was the chap who had published his own books about his sex tour, books I had declined to sell. *Bonkinq in Bangkok* is number one in the paperback bestseller list, having sold 52,000 copies in its first week.

Memo to self: Can't you get anything right?

Tuesday 11 May

A somewhat chastened Paul Ross sidled into the shop this afternoon. The last time I saw him he was shouting at me after the Thacker inquest, but today he was all meekness and goodwill. I had high hopes of shifting a few tomes from the religious shelf, given his predilections – the thoughts of Billy Graham, a life of Martin Luther, the inside dope on the post-Aids, anti-condom Vatican, or even a thin tract we have here from the Aetherius Society who believe that Jesus lives on Venus and rides around in a flying saucer. But he hadn't come in to spend money.

'Something terrible happened this morning,' he said.

'What?' I said quickly, fearful that it involved Marisa.

'You remember the car accident Andrew had? He was in court this morning and they've banned him for two years.'

'He's very lucky,' I said. 'He drove when he was hopelessly drunk and nearly killed somebody. He should have been locked up.'

'He has a drink problem,' Paul said. 'You have to be sympathetic.'

'Not if he's in a car, I don't.'

'The thing is,' he went on, looking quite amazingly uneasy, 'certain things follow from his disqualification.'

'Like what?' I asked. I still felt cheated at yet another person coming in who hadn't even thought about buying a book.

He gave me a strange look. 'What are your intentions so far as Marisa is concerned?'

'What's that got to do with it?'

'Quite a lot. You see, Andrew can't drive his old Honda over to my house to see me, so he wants to move in.'

'Do you want him to move in?'

'Yes, I do.'

So you want Marisa to move out, I thought. The selfishness of it was mind-boggling, but I felt a warm glow at the prospect that was opening up.

'Do you want to marry Marisa?' he asked. It sounded offensive, as if he were trying to off-load her.

'I'd have married her years ago if you hadn't intervened,' I told him. He said nothing and looked at the floor. 'At the moment I'm married to someone else.'

'Yes, I know. But if you wanted to marry Marisa there would be no problem from me so far as the divorce is concerned.'

It was good to hear this, but I didn't say so. The trouble was my divorce, not his.

'Does Marisa know you're here?' I asked.

'Credit me with some discretion,' he replied. 'I was hoping that you and I could make certain decisions.' He looked at me hopefully, but I wasn't about to reassure him. Marisa and I would sort out our future ourselves, and I began to resent the way that he was placing himself centre stage, and trying to organize the lives of other people.

'Any decisions I make will be with Marisa,' I said. 'I'm sure she'll let you know.'

'I just wanted you to understand the situation,' he said mildly. 'It's not easy.'

'You've made your decision, Paul. Now you've got to live with it.'

'But I'm right in thinking that you want to marry Marisa? I need to know that much.'

'You're right,' I told him.

He nodded and walked out of the shop towards a future that I couldn't bear to contemplate.

Wednesday 12 May

I wrote to Emma and phoned Marisa. My frantic attempts now to sort out my private life were beginning to fill my working day. I didn't even have time to invent verse.

That moving picture of you in the newspaper snogging the rakish

Rupert clutched my heart, I wrote to Emma. *My solicitor was overcome by emotion as well. 'Why doesn't she marry the debonair clown?' he sobbed. Only joking. But my friend Marisa would like to move in here with me, and it's certainly what I want. However, she is inhibited by the thought that you might suddenly reappear. Can you put us all out of our misery by telling us what your intentions are? Hutton.*

I had to phone Marisa three times before she was able to talk: his lordship was prowling the premises, choosing paintings for a future exhibition.

'I've had a visit from your husband,' I said.

'In the shop? What did he say?'

'Get your dirty paws off my woman, or I'll blow your legs off.'

'What did he say?' she repeated.

'He said Andrew, the drunken driver, has been banned for two years and so can't drive over to see his boyfriend every day.'

'Oh, good.'

'No, bad. He wants Andrew to be his permanent house guest now that he can't travel.'

'Oh God, no,' said Marisa and went silent. 'I couldn't stand that,' she said, after thinking about the prospect that was being offered to her. 'You've got to save me from this.'

'And I will,' I said. 'There's a nice house in Trebor Avenue that is waiting for your arrival.' I imagined in my naivety that this was an irresistible proposition given the impending arrival of Andrew Burrows; I'd forgotten that the Emma problem would still be there.

'We've covered this ground before,' she reminded me. 'I can't just move into your house and sit there like a cuckoo. I need to know that Emma is seeking a divorce, otherwise she could just turn up and resent my presence.'

'I think she's too busy kissing Rupert for that,' I said, frightened by her tone. 'I've written to Emma this morning, asking what her plans are. I've told her that I want you to move here, and let her know I'd seen the newspaper story.'

'That kiss could have been quite innocent.'

'The story didn't suggest it.' But I was worried that my letter to the Isle of Man would produce a long silence, followed by the evasion and frustration of her last reply. 'If necessary I'll fly out and see her,' I promised.

Wednesday 19 May

Instead of a reply from Emma, a letter arrives from Luke.

Dear Mark,

Greetings from Down Under! I thought I'd written my last letter to you, but as I'm dealing with lawyers on two fronts (1. The divorce. 2. The business settlement) things are taking longer than I expected, and I reckon I'll be here for three weeks. Nicole had assured me that everything would be decided amicably, but I'm lumbered with a rapacious lawyer who seems to think that I'm ripping her off. We have shouting matches on the twelfth floor of his Brisbane office. He's come up from Tasmania because he thinks that this is where the money is, and he's too dim to realize that Nicole and I have already agreed about the distribution of the family assets. He secretly believes that he will enhance his own fee if he clips something off what I'm supposed to get. I may have to kill him. One moron less – it's a public service.

Nicole has treated me with great kindness since I arrived here (although we sleep in separate rooms) and says the mad lawyer is just part of the game we are playing. I have to be honest I wasn't looking for a divorce, but Nicole obviously had it in her mind from way back. She said the other day that she was relieved when I agreed to it. I said, 'I always agree with you, Nicole. I find it makes life easier', and she said, 'Perhaps that was the trouble.'

What do you make of that?

It's autumn here now. Winter starts 1 June. But the weather is good. I sit and read the Courier-Mail but nothing much is happening here. Shirley Bassey's 50th anniversary tour is about to reach the Brisbane Convention and Exhibition Centre but I might not make that.

But none of this is why I'm writing. The purpose of this letter is to update you on an interesting development.

I was standing in the front room a couple of days ago, staring out of the window and wondering how to fill the time, when a taxi pulled up outside – and Jamie got out! He looked very smart in a new brown suit, but had little luggage.

As it happened, Nicole was out at the shops so it fell to me to open the door to him. He looked stunned. I was fairly surprised myself.

'What the hell are you doing here?' I asked.

'Nicole invited me', he said. 'I didn't expect to find you here.'

'Life is full of surprises', I said. 'Come in.'

It was an odd situation as you can guess. Jamie was actually embarrassed which is a hard thing to imagine. I fixed him a drink and asked whether this was a flying visit or whether he planned to stay.

'That's rather up to Nicole', he said, 'but if you're asking me whether I'd sooner live in a shed the answer's No.'

Nicole's face was a picture when she came back and found us chatting in the kitchen, but she was obviously delighted to see him. It turned out that she had posted Jamie an open air ticket, but didn't know whether or when he would use it. I'd sent an e-

mail to her the day before I flew, but there was no way she could contact Jamie to tell him. He can't receive e-mails and he hasn't got a phone.

So there we were, the three of us, with me an unwelcome guest at this romantic reunion.

Yesterday Jamie said, 'You're all right about this, aren't you, Luke? After all, you are getting a divorce.'

It was difficult to explain that, divorce or no divorce, it was painful to have this stuff going on under your nose.

Last night we all went out to dinner at one of Brisbane's finest. Luckily there were several legal matters that Nicole and I had to discuss so I wasn't entirely excluded from the conversation. But there was also plenty of cosy chat and giggles between the two of them. I could see how it works. To the girl from Brisbane, Jamie is urbane, sophisticated, worldly-wise. He may have no money but he's seen more of the world than any of us. His trade is pleasing women. To the boy from the shed living on pasta and brown rice, Nicole offers him everything he needs – money, a house, company, freedom from an impoverished lifestyle, wonderful food.

But it's all pretty unexpected, isn't it? I remember saying to you that it was only a holiday affair in which she was using him as a man-about-London. How little I know about her – which may account for the break-up of my marriage.

I took him for a lunch drink at a local bar today. We've overcome the embarrassment of his arrival now and accept the situation. He asked a lot of questions about Nicole, her past and how she started the business. I felt he was boning up on a subject he needed to thoroughly understand, and whose interests he intends to share. What a professional!

Now I've got to spend a few depressing days going through my possessions in this house and seeing what I want to ship to England. When I left the country last time I thought I'd only be away for a few weeks. I expect I'll find this exploration of the past rather sad, but I'm in a sad mood at the moment. I suppose what really pisses me off is that they sleep together, but as I'm about to be divorced I'm hardly in a position to complain.

I'll be in touch when I get back to England.

Cheers,

Luke

Wednesday 26 May

She's here! The angel has landed!

The doorbell rang just after eight this evening and as usual I was in two minds about whether to answer it. But after the unexpected arrival of Jamie Croft I decided I would.

Marisa stood on the step surrounded by suitcases. She threw her arms round my neck and burst into tears.

'Oh Mark, I can't stand it,' she said.

I lifted her up and carried her over the threshold – there was something very symbolic about this – and then I kissed her and calmed her down. I fetched her suitcases, locked the door and guided her into the sitting-room.

'I'm not letting you go,' I told her.

'I don't want to go. God, it was awful.'

We sat on the sofa, snuggled up together. By an extraordinary stroke of good fortune I had spent the last hour and more cleaning the house. I had hoovered carpets, dusted shelves, cleaned work surfaces in the kitchen and, best of all, put clean sheets on the bed. It was an unusual display of housewifely behaviour, but it couldn't have been better timed.

'Tell me about it,' I said.

She was wearing pink jeans and a pale-blue T-shirt with a fawn on the front. She had obviously changed when she got home from the gallery. Her face was sad but this didn't disguise how lovely it was. I had to kiss her.

'Thank you,' she said. It seemed strange to be thanked for a kiss, but she was grateful to be pulled up from her depression. 'Andrew moved in on Sunday,' she explained. 'I didn't want it but I couldn't stop it. I thought that when I was there they would behave normally and for a couple of days they did. But by yesterday things had changed. Homosexuality turns out to be a very tactile business. They were constantly touching each other, touching and stroking. But tonight they kissed – you know, on the mouth. That was enough for me. Good luck to them, but I couldn't bear to watch it. This man used to be my husband.'

She was staring rather sadly at my newly hoovered carpet, reliving, perhaps, this indiscreet moment.

'They were pretty inconsiderate, weren't they?'

She shrugged. 'They wanted me to go, and it worked. I left the room and started to pack everything I could into my suitcases. I had to leave some stuff behind, but I'll pick it up one day. I threw the cases into the Golf and drove here as fast as I could.'

'Thank God you did,' I said. 'Have you eaten?'

'I have, but I'd love a drink.'

'It'll have to be champagne,' I said, 'unless you'd like canned beer.'

'Why have you got champagne? Do you celebrate on your own?'

'It's been waiting for you.'

I poured the drinks and then gave her a guided tour of the house. Upstairs I transferred Emma's stuff to the wardrobe in the guest bedroom to provide space for the contents of Marisa's suitcases.

'It's nice. I could live here,' she said, as she hung up her clothes. 'You've even got clean sheets on the bed!'

We went downstairs and finished the champagne. I was looking round uneasily for any embarrassing mementoes that might be on display – there had for years been a framed photograph of Emma and me grinning inanely outside the register office, but I was relieved and surprised to see that it had gone. I hadn't noticed before. I don't imagine that Emma took it with her to the Isle of Man. She must have ditched it as part of the New Year's Day farewell.

'No news from Emma then?' Marisa asked, uncannily echoing my thoughts.

'Not yet,' I admitted. 'Boy, have I got news for her!'

'The question is, how is she going to take it?'

'As phlegmatically as I took her kissing picture in the *Daily Mail*,' I said. 'It's over, Marisa. Get her out of your head. Would you like a coffee?'

'I'd love one.'

'And after that we're going upstairs to make love if I can remember how to do it.'

'You might have to jog my memory.'

We went into the kitchen laughing to make coffee. There are two things you never forget and one of them is how to ride a bicycle.

And two hours later between the crisp, clean sheets Marisa whispered in my ear, 'You *did* remember!'

Memo to self: Well done.

JUNE

Summer heat, late afternoon tea,
provincial gossip, yawns barely hidden.
– *J.M Coetzee*

Tuesday 1 June

It came as an unpleasant shock to discover that Marisa would have to get up before me to leave for her job in London. My work is only a mile away.

The answer, obviously, is for her to give up the art gallery. After all, she had only taken it on to augment the family income when her husband became a part-time traffic warden. Surely the money from the bookshop would make her daily trip to London unnecessary?

I had to remind myself that Emma had never found the shop's profits entirely satisfactory, and they were lower now. I wanted Marisa to give up work, but could I afford it? I decided that before I talked to her I would talk to my bank manager.

Colin Newman greeted me warmly in his starkly furnished office. His welcome was understandable. Whether I was making money or losing it Colin Newman was making money out of me. I had an overdraft limit of £10,000 which I made plentiful use of, but the interest he charged me always seemed to be higher than the figure I saw mentioned in the newspapers.

'How's business?' he asked, when I had sat down in front of his green desk.

'It has been better,' I said. 'Can people still read?'

'There used to be a rather good song called "Video Killed the Radio Star". Now it's video killed the literary star?'

'There's a lot of competition for people's attention,' I conceded.

That was the end of the small talk. He stared at me across the desk. 'What can I do for you?' he asked. He wore old-fashioned horn-rimmed spectacles and always reminded me of one of those characters in the Carry On films.

'I want you to double my overdraft limit,' I said. I didn't feel obliged to explain.

'I don't see why not,' he said. 'You've got more security than most people.'

'I have?'

'You own a house with the mortgage paid off. You own a shop that's paid for, and it's got a flat above, hasn't it?'

The picture he painted cheered me up. I was beginning to regard the shop as a poor investment, but, of course, property is king. I left the bank with an unfamiliar sense of prosperity.

'Quit work, kid,' I said to Marisa over dinner. 'All that going up and down to London isn't good for you.' Dinner was a prawn salad that I had lovingly prepared: it was on the outer limit of my culinary expertise.

'Don't we need the money?' she asked. 'I'd love to pack it up. I could cook your dinner then. It would be nice to prepare something that wasn't spaghetti.'

'We don't need the money,' I assured her. 'I'm not a part-time traffic warden.'

'What about Emma? Doesn't she have a claim on your millions?'

'My wife is a successful self-supporting actress, I'm glad to say. She has her own bank account and hasn't asked for a penny this year.'

'In that case,' said Marisa, 'I'll have a word with his lordship. But I'll probably have to do another month or two while he finds a replacement.'

'How will he do that?' I asked. 'You're irreplaceable.'

Wednesday 2 June

Things get better and better. Today a letter arrived from Emma and it contained all the news I wanted to hear.

Dear Hutton
I'm sorry for the delay in replying to your letter. There were things to sort out here. I'm now reasonably confident that my future lies with Rupert, but I will need to make one last visit to Trebor Avenue to clear out my things. I'll give you warning of this so that Marisa can be out. Have you really talked to a solicitor? If we both want a divorce do we need to deal with those greedy freaks? I know I have rights in the house but given your ongoing poverty and my startling film expectations, I'm happy to sacrifice them. I don't want you living in the street. I hope we can meet and talk as friends at the Westacotts' party when I shall introduce you to Rupert and you can introduce me to Marisa. Didn't you know a girl called Marisa at school? Fancy you meeting two girls with the same unusual name!
Emma Hutton (aka Emma Benson)

The change this letter produced in Marisa was wonderful to behold. I think she had been holding back, half-expecting Emma to walk through the door and reclaim her rights. But now she threw her arms round me and couldn't stop smiling. Her relief was obvious; the future was real.

'You mustn't tell her it's the same Marisa,' she said. 'She'll think you've been carrying a torch for me.'

'I have.'

'It will be hurtful for her. Take advice from a woman.'

Memo to self: I will.

Monday 7 June

Luke, newly enriched from the dissolution of his marriage and physically strengthened by his prolonged absence from the attentions of Shirley Burrows, bounced into the shop like a gazelle. Celibacy had made him look younger, or at least removed the drained expression he had been wearing when I last saw him, and he seemed to have been rejuvenated by his arguments in Australia.

'I'm free!' he announced, with both hands raised above his head in a gesture of victory. 'I'll never see Nicole or Australia again.'

'The classless society.'

'Yes – no class. And as for Nicole, being married to her was a minefield. The trouble was she was the only person who knew where the mines were planted.'

'So where are you living?'

'I'm back in the Walton Hall. They were pleased to see me and my wallet.'

'I bet they were. How's Jamie getting on Down Under?'

'He's really taken to it. I wonder how long it'll last?'

'A long time,' I said. 'Where else can he go?'

I made him the obligatory coffee and we sat down.

'What have I missed?' he asked.

'Quite a lot, actually,' I told him. 'There have been a few developments in your absence.'

'Like?'

'The first thing that happened was that Andrew was banned from driving for two years after his crash on the night of Thacker's death. And so, as he couldn't drive over to see his new boyfriend Paul Ross, he moved in with him.'

'What did Marisa say to that?'

'She put up with it until they started kissing, and then she moved out. She lives with me now.'

Luke's face split into a satisfied grin. 'That's wonderful,' he said.

'It certainly is – particularly as Emma appears to have found a new man.'

The grin that had occupied Luke's face slowly metamorphosed into a deep frown. 'Just a minute,' he said. 'This game of sexual musical chairs seems to have left a vacant chair.'

'I thought you'd spot that.'

'Shirley is living alone?'

'It's tragic really,' I said. 'All that sexual energy going to waste.'

He drained his coffee and stood up. 'See you,' he said, and shot out of the shop like a dog which has just caught the scent of a fox.

Friday 18 June

We've been to the theatre (Stoppard), we've caught up on a couple of films (Curtis, Minghella), and we've dined in some well-run local restaurants that I'd never been in before. But tonight our appointment was with a newly engaged couple who live in a detached house on a pleasant estate twenty miles away. Our hosts greeted us with wild enthusiasm.

'Marisa!' screamed Luke, giving her a hug. Shirley Burrows (née Appleton and soon, apparently, to be Dyson) hugged her, too. The three of them knew each other from schooldays, but it was years since Marisa had seen either.

Forewarned about the dramatic change in Shirley's appearance, Marisa handled it with the ease I expected. 'Shirley, you look lovely,' she said. 'What are you doing with this Australian reject?'

'Training him,' said Shirley with a Monroe-like giggle.

'What's this about marriage?' I asked Luke, as we went into the house. He had mentioned their plans when he rang with the invitation.

'We're getting married two seconds after Shirley gets her decree,' he said. 'Which should be a fairly straightforward procedure as her husband's buggering a traffic warden.'

'Speed the whole thing up no end, I imagine.'

The home into which Luke had effortlessly slipped must have been furnished during Andrew's profitable years: it was not the house of a bankrupt. Luke led the way to a luxurious drinks cabinet and waved some bottle in my face. To his surprise I chose beer.

'I'm driving Marisa,' I explained.

'You used to drive home from the Walton Hall after a gallon of whisky,' he protested.

'I was younger then.'

He poured me a San Miguel and then took a bottle of wine to the kitchen from which came the sound of Shirley and Marisa laughing, and the smell of fine food. It was a home-made steak and kidney pie with superb pastry and four vegetables. It appeared through a serving hatch that linked the dining-room to the kitchen and was carried by Luke to the table that was already laid.

Shirley, sporting a little white dress tonight that looked as if it needed another, larger dress over it, turned out to be a fascinating hostess. She had no compunction about divulging the details of her sexual career which had begun with somebody called Ben Giffard in a Brighton bus shelter and then burgeoned rapidly beneath the hedgerows of the South Downs. Her motto from an early age had been 'if you can't be good, be good at it' and in her more mature years she had honed and perfected skills that had allegedly dumped one man in a wheelchair, and driven the latest to the hazards of sodomy. Another former lover had gone bald overnight, while an earlier recipient of her efforts had been carted from the London Marathon on a stretcher after only one mile.

My suspicion that this frank narrative might frighten the socks off Luke proved ill-founded; he looked increasingly like the man who has won the Lottery.

Shirley herself had emerged from her scabrous endeavours with energy to spare. She now funnelled her vitality into a variety of activities: part-time teaching to five year olds, charity work with meals-on-wheels, nursery minding, and helping out at some local stables.

'I think you deserve a medal,' said Marisa, 'although I'm not quite sure what the inscription would say.'

'She gave a hundred per cent,' said Luke. 'A heroine of our times.' He refilled his wine glass and looked pleased at his dedication.

Marisa turned to him, curious perhaps about a man who was prepared to take on this dynamo. 'What do you do, Luke?' she asked. 'I gather you sit at your computer and play with money?' Her expression suggested as tactfully as possible that this was not an adequate preparation for the physical demands that were about to ambush him in the bedroom.

'Stocks and shares,' said Luke. 'Buying and selling.'

'Is that very profitable?'

'I turned ten grand into thirty-five in a month once, but it's a swings and roundabouts game. What you need is a little nerve and a lot of information. What you must do is avoid the Web.'

'Why's that?'

'Have you heard of pump and dump?'

'It sounds familiar,' said Shirley drily.

'People with failing shares put messages on the Internet saying how promising they are. The folks who read this rush out to buy them and the price goes up. You pump up the value and then sell them.'

'I hope you don't do anything so discreditable,' said Marisa.

'Not me.'

'Luke's speciality,' I said, 'is reorganizing people's lives. The domestic rearrangements that have flowed directly from his decision to fly to Britain at the beginning of the year are quite extraordinary.'

We looked at each other across the table, the proof of what I had said.

'I think I've sorted everybody out,' Luke said proudly.

Memo to self: I think he has, too.

JULY

The English winter – ending in July
To recommence in August.
– *Lord Byron*

Saturday 3 July

The engraved invitation from the newly ennobled Lord and Lady Westacott was addressed to 'Mark Hutton and partner', a refinement that had no doubt been instigated by Emma. Marisa was delighted. She liked the idea of a garden party and was curious about meeting my wife.

The setting was extraordinary. Most of the Westacotts' two acres were laid to lawn and at the centre of it stood a gigantic marquee. In here was a free bar and a homemade kitchen in which two chefs were slaving over food. There were tables and chairs for those who wanted to eat and drink inside, but many more on the lawn for those who wanted to enjoy a perfect summer evening. The focal point of the occasion was a dance band that played in a corner of the grounds, with a dance floor laid over the lawn in front of them.

There were probably more than 150 carefully chosen guests milling around in the garden and a security guard at the gate had checked our invitations to make sure that there were no unwanted ones. Wandering into this extravaganza I seemed to be surrounded by half-forgotten faces of people who had achieved temporary celebrity in my life: a once-famous model of elegant slimness who now sadly appeared gaunt, an actor from a film that I had enjoyed whose hairy persona had succumbed to the ravages of time – there was now hardly any hair at all, and a couple of MPs whose noisy interventions in the Commons contrasted oddly with their docile demeanour tonight as they stood silently beside their wives. Marisa thought that she spotted Prince Harry but I think she was mistaken.

'First thing we do,' I said, after studying our impressive surroundings, 'is get a drink.'

'That's exactly what you said to me the last time you took me to a party,' said Marisa.

'That was light ale, this is champagne.'

In the marquee we bumped into Janet.

'This is some party,' I told her.

'Isn't it wonderful?' she replied.

'I'd like you to meet Marisa. Marisa, this is Lady Westacott.'

'Hallo dear,' said Janet. 'You two must come and talk to Emma and her friend Rupert. I'll show you where they're sitting.' I had the feeling that she was under instruction to deliver us to their table.

Six months in the enchanted world of movies had transformed my wife. Her hair had been cut shorter and streaked. Her wide eyes had picked up tricks from the make-up artists that made her look more attractive. She was wearing a purple flowing dress that I had not seen before.

I kissed this stranger on the cheek and she turned to Rupert. 'This is Mark, who always puts the chicken in the oven upside down.'

Rupert, a rather handsome man with black wavy hair that was grey at the temples – he was 45, I remembered, according to the *Daily Mail* – shook my hand and I introduced Marisa to both of them.

'Watch his DIY, Marisa,' said Emma. 'He once built a bird table that keeled over when a sparrow landed on it.' Everybody laughed.

'I can see my shortcomings are going to be a source of humour,' I said. 'Anyway, it was a blackbird.'

We sat down with our drinks and discussed the film they had now finished. There was some cutting and editing to be done, but *The Devil's Spouse*, we were told, was scheduled to reach the cinemas in the autumn.

Reluctantly I rather took to Rupert. A considerable talent aligned to genuine modesty is an appealing combination. He leaned towards me and muttered: 'This all seems a bit lavish for a Labour MP, doesn't it?'

'Do you remember Robert Maxwell?' I asked.

'Do I not! Maxwell, Archer, Hamilton, Aitken – we *schadenfreudians* had never had it so good.'

'You never know who has the money these days,' Marisa said. 'I was stopped by a beggar in Soho last week and a mobile phone went off in his pocket.'

'He'd probably stolen it,' said Rupert.

'Well he answered it.'

We were joined suddenly by Phoebe Davenport, dressed tonight in subfusc charity shop gear. To my surprise she knew Rupert Barkley, but the surprise was ratcheted up to mind-numbing stupefaction when Emma explained why.

Phoebe had sent proofs of her novel to Emma in the Isle of Man after I had given her the address, and Emma, loving the book, had shown it to Rupert. He had become very excited about its cinematic possibilities and invited Phoebe over. He then made what Emma described in the language of the business as a pre-emptive six-figure bid for the film rights before anybody else could read it. Phoebe signed the contract in a pub in Douglas. She was certainly exultant tonight as she had every reason to be.

The schmaltzy music had produced in Marisa the urge to dance and we went off for a spin.

'Emma's nice,' she said, as we manoeuvred our way through the swaying revellers.

'I hope she stays that way,' I whispered. 'I'll have to talk to her later on.'

'Phoebe's a bit odd though. She found it necessary to tell me that sixty-eight per cent of murdered women are killed by their husbands.'

'A bee in her bonnet. She's mad as a balloon.'

After the dance we took a stroll around the grounds. I was glad to see that the koi carp were surviving in the pond despite the hostile herons. In the evening sun several guests were describing the scene to less fortunate friends on mobile phones. A rock star from another era lurched into us.

'I've lost the bar,' he said.

'It's in the tent,' I told him. His young girlfriend wore a yellow T-shirt which bore the legend IT'S HARD BEING THIS BEAUTIFUL.

I decided to head for the marquee myself. The only thing this party lacked was waiter service with the drinks. We ran into Charles Westacott *en route*. A woman with a face like a haddock and a voice that sounded as if she had just inhaled helium was complaining to him about the wanton promiscuity of the young. Perhaps she thought he could do something about it in the House of Lords.

'A churlish remark coming from a woman who is rarely vertical,' he said, when she had moved on.

'You're not telling me that creature has a sex life?' I asked incredulously.

'The world's full of myopic men with appetites,' said Charles with the new authority society had handed him. 'Enjoying yourself?'

'It's wonderful, Charles,' I told him. 'Your generosity is amazing.'

He laughed happily and hurried away.

In the marquee people were exploring the epicurean

delights of the Westacotts' hospitality. Marisa ended up dipping sushi in soy sauce, but I was happy with more champagne and I drank while she ate.

When we finally got back to the table we discovered that Phoebe was facing another title change for her novel. Rupert could not see *How To Bin Your Husband* as a good title for a film, although suitable for 'the catchpenny world of paperbacks.'

'Movies are more cerebral,' he said. 'We're appealing to a different audience.'

'So what do you suggest?' Phoebe asked.

'How about – this is off the top of my head – *Hounding Husbands*?'

'That wouldn't do at all,' Phoebe replied instantly. 'It puts women in the wrong which isn't where I'm coming from.'

'This woman in your novel – what's her name? Maggie Radford – displays a certain impatience with men.'

'The men in my novel give her every reason to do so.'

'I'm playing Maggie Radford,' Emma now revealed. 'Impatience towards men I can handle.'

'I spent years nurturing that side of her,' I said. 'What's in it for me?'

Rupert laughed. 'You could have a credit at the end of the film. Impatience nurturer – Mark Hutton.' He then tried to explain to Phoebe as gently as possible that she had sold the film rights of her novel and it was now out of her hands.

'Scriptwriters will get to work on it in the next few weeks and they have a lot of licence. They'll change things that you've done, and then I'll appear on the scene and change things they've done.'

'And in the end my novel will be unrecognizable.'

'Take the money and run,' I advised.

'The heart of it will be there. You'll get a big credit. Read your contract. Based on a novel by Phoebe Davenport.'

Phoebe did not look happy but she took my advice. 'I think I'd better shut up,' she said. 'Emma as Maggie Radford would be lovely.'

The women left us soon after this – why do they always go together? – and I asked Rupert what he thought of her.

'She's got a low drag-coefficient,' he said. I had to look it up afterwards. He meant she'd got a low bum. 'But she's a bright girl,' he added. 'She's got a very interesting mind. How are things in the bookselling world in this post-Gutenborgian era? You're buggered with a capital F, aren't you?'

'More or less,' I admitted.

'I'm glad I'm in movies. They're the future. There was a nasty moment a few years ago when we all thought that television was the future, but then television got worse and films got better.'

'I remember,' I said. 'Why did that happen?'

'Television couldn't afford it, and we could. Television is like one of those old–fashioned nationalized industries, struggling to balance the books. There was over a billion invested in British films last year.'

'And how is Emma going to do,' I asked, 'in Phoebe's film?'

'She'll be a sensation. She's got a rare natural talent that I've seldom seen.'

The possessor of this rare natural talent approached the table and beckoned me. I stood up and went over to her, and then we sauntered solemnly around the grounds thinking about our futures.

'Marisa's nice,' Emma told me with a hint of surprise.

'She said the same thing about you.'

'You must marry her.'

'What a good idea. Has Rupert proposed yet?'

'Not yet, but he will.' Her new career had given her a confidence that she hadn't always had. 'Good God!' she said. 'Isn't that—?'

She was looking at a pop idol of her youth who was sitting at a table on the lawn with his family.

'Yes, it is,' I said. 'Don't worry – he'll soon be a fan of yours.'

We went into the marquee for a drink. There was no sign of the champagne running out. We took a table, and Emma said, 'I've made a discovery.'

The new image she had brought with her tonight looked pretty good under the marquee's gentle lights, and you could see how the camera would love her.

'What's that?' I asked.

'Divorce on the Internet. Quickie Divorce UK. Not a solicitor in sight.'

'It sounds good,' I said, 'but I don't have a computer.'

'I have access to one. Leave it to me. They can settle uncontested divorces without a court appearance and at minimal cost. Last year more than five-thousand people got divorced using the Internet.'

'What grounds do they want?' I asked. It was amazing how little I knew about divorce. The picture it had always evoked for me was of a shoddy detective hovering outside a hotel bedroom in Brighton.

'There are five,' said Emma, who had obviously been doing some research. 'Adultery, unreasonable behaviour, two-year separation with consent, five-year separation, and desertion. I think it'll have to be adultery, don't you?'

'Go for it,' I said. It wasn't clear whether she meant mine or hers.

'After the decree nisi you have to wait six weeks and one day for the decree absolute. Then you're free to marry.'

'And it'll all be done online? Welcome to the twenty-first century.'

'I knew I'd get you there one day,' said Emma.

Thursday 8 July

Mrs Pringle descended from her eyrie this morning to impart unwelcome news. She wants to go. Guilt flickered across her face as she told me this, as if she were reneging on a promise, but of course there was no reason why she shouldn't leave.

'I'm sorry, Mark,' she said, 'but I'm not getting any younger and I've been lonely ever since I lost my husband. My widowed sister, who has a lovely house in Bournemouth, has been saying for years that we would make company for each other.'

It was a double blow to me. At a stroke I was going to lose my able deputy and the rent from the flat upstairs.

'I'm sorry you're going,' I said, 'but I can see it will be best for you. Bournemouth's a nice place.'

She seemed relieved at my approval. 'I won't leave until the end of August,' she assured me. 'I'll let the holiday crowds thin out first.'

When I gave Marisa the news this evening her reaction was immediate. 'We must have a holiday before she goes. I'm leaving the gallery on August 6. We could do it then. Once Mrs Pringle has gone holidays will be impossible to arrange.'

'Good idea,' I said. 'France? Spain? The Caribbean?'

But Marisa had another idea. 'I'm too old to lie in the sun. What we ought to do is visit my parents in Dorchester so I can explain my new situation.'

I wasn't sure that such a meeting would provide the calm and relaxation that I associated with holidays, but I could see that it was a necessary development.

'Arrange it,' I said.

Wednesday 14 July

It is a truth universally acknowledged that if you share a house with someone you will end up watching television programmes that you don't really want to see. But this was a minor sacrifice when you had the company of Marisa. Snuggled up with her on the sofa I could happily have gazed at Shakespeare in Japanese.

Tonight she was gripped by the umpteenth trawl through the life of Diana, the story of the Spencer dynasty and the disputes that followed her death. It was hard to believe that there was anything new to say on the subject, but the media kept discovering things or making them up and in Marisa they had a ready audience.

In these early days I still feel like a host and am careful not to disturb her concentration. But the commercial break permitted conversation and the information she was about to pass on gave me a considerable jolt.

'It's my birthday on Sunday week,' she said.

'Is it?' I said. 'What are you going to let me buy you?'

It was not surprising that I didn't know when her birthday was. They hadn't meant much when we were young and were largely ignored. On 1 April she hadn't known that it was mine.

'I'm not looking for a present,' she said. 'It's a bit more important than that.'

I looked at her questioningly.

'It's a little tradition,' she said. 'My son always comes to lunch on my birthday. So I thought I'd invite him here.'

'Blimey,' I said. 'Gosh, yes.'

'The news seems to have reduced you to incoherence,' Marisa said with a laugh. 'You can meet your son!'

'That would be terrific,' I said, repelling an attack of nerves.

'And I'm going to tell him,' Marisa said, 'who his father really is.'

Memo to self: Calm down!

Sunday 25 July

I bought Marisa a Gucci watch which cost more than a thousand pounds. Such extravagance has become possible now that my overdraft limit has been doubled. I took her breakfast in bed and then lay on it and we talked. The truth was that I was trying to delay high noon, to push it into the future. My son was arriving at twelve o'clock and I found the prospect strangely disturbing.

'I don't mind being forty-nine,' said Marisa. 'It's next year I'm not looking forward to.'

'You look thirty-nine,' I told her, and it was true.

The watch, an oblong shaped model with no numbers but tiny diamonds down each side, cost £1,275 which was more than the Dior or Versace that an eager jeweller produced for my inspection. Marisa loved it.

When she got up I helped her prepare the vegetables that would go with the roast beef that was to be the centre of the birthday Sunday lunch.

'I think you should open the door to him,' Marisa suggested. 'That way I won't have to introduce you.'

She had put a picture of him on the mantelpiece and I picked it up and studied it. Then I looked in the mirror to see what my son would see. The same alert eyes, the same nose – even the combed-back hair was similar, although he had more than I had.

'He's a good-looking man,' I said. 'He looks just like me.'

'Modesty was never your bag,' said Marisa. 'Do you think he'll notice?'

'I don't see how he can miss it.'

I put the picture back and dumped some champagne in an ice bucket. Then I returned to my potato-peeling duties and wondered what on earth I was going to say to him. If Mark had been in his teens I could have handled it easily, but a psychiatrist of thirty-one was a more difficult assignment. And the possibility of embarrassment didn't end with the paternity question; there was also the way that I had installed Marisa in my house like some absconding tart.

'What do I call him?' I asked. 'Mark? Doctor Ross? Sir? There's going to be a surfeit of Marks in here today.'

'I'll call him dear, and you darling, darling. You can call each other Mark.'

'Do you call your father Mark?'

'You do if you don't know he's your father.'

There were other worries that I wanted to discuss. 'How is he going to react to our set-up here?'

'He's perfectly relaxed about it. I've explained that you were my boyfriend before I met Paul. He thinks it's rather romantic. Also he knows about Paul's exciting new sexual inclinations so he's sympathetic about my move.' She looked at her new watch. 'According to my wonderful birthday present it's twelve o'clock.'

The doorbell rang immediately.

'That's his ring,' Marisa said. 'Off you go.'

The man who faced me on the doorstep was better looking than the photograph over the fireplace. He had inherited the best parts of his mother's good looks, particularly the eyes. He was dressed casually in brown slacks and an expensive-looking blue check shirt that was open at the neck. He had a slim athletic build, and was clutching a bunch of freesias.

'Mark Hutton?' he said, extending his hand. 'It's good to meet you.'

'Come in, come in,' I said, still uncertain what to call him.

He stepped into the hall with his flowers and said, 'How's Mum?' He had the clear, classless voice that often comes out of good schools.

'Wonderful, as always.'

He showed me the flowers. 'Her favourite,' he said. 'She loves the smell.'

I reproached myself for not knowing this. Marisa was waiting with a hug and a kiss. 'Freesias!' she said, as if her son had brought gold ingots. 'Come in, dear, and grab a drink.'

'Happy birthday,' he said, taking a glass of champagne and clinking glasses.

'I hope so,' said Marisa, looking at me. 'Why don't you two sit down with your drinks while I dish up?' She was afraid that we would offer to help her when what she wanted was for us to get to know each other. I led my son to the dining-room where the table was laid.

'That's some job you've got,' I said, groping for a subject. Luckily he was happy to discuss it.

'It's more interesting than some,' he said, maintaining an eye-to-eye contact which was vaguely disconcerting, but probably formed an intrinsic part of his professional armoury. 'It keeps me busy, and that's the main thing. Crime marches on, taking mental illness with it. Ten years ago we hadn't heard of a stalker. Twenty years ago you never heard the word paedophile. Now every other person I deal with is one or the other, and some versatile folk are both. There are people out there, pioneers in their way, doing things we haven't put a name to yet.'

'It's frightening.'

'It's business.'

When Marisa started to bring in the food Mark produced his present, an expensively framed photograph of her grandson. I helped carry food and delivered red and white wine to the table not even knowing whether my son drank.

'That's a lovely picture,' said Marisa, when we were sitting down. She had accorded it a place of honour on the mantelpiece, next to her son. 'What a good-looking boy he is.' The warm family feeling generated by this remark probably prompted Mark's next question, and suddenly the floodgates of disclosure opened.

'How is my bi-sexual father?' he asked. 'And how has he taken this move?'

Marisa, seeing an opening, plunged in.

'There's something I have to tell you, dear. I should have told you before, but I kept thinking that I would wait until you were older.'

'And thirty-one is old enough? What is it? Something about Santa Claus?'

'It's worse than that. Paul isn't your father.'

I admired the way that she had gone straight to the point, but wondered whether a roundabout route would have been preferable. Our son looked at her, laughed and nodded.

'I know that, Mum,' he said. 'It's a subject I was going to bring up with you but, like you, I kept postponing the day.'

'You *know* it? How can you possibly know it? *He* doesn't know it.'

I imagined our son digging among the archives at Somerset House, or wherever family records were kept these days, but what could he learn there? The father's name on his birth certificate was Paul Ross.

'I suspected it,' he said, 'and so I found out. I'm a seeker after the truth.'

Marisa took this information in and frowned. 'May I ask why you doubted it?'

Mark considered it, and then answered with the detail a

doctor would bring to a complex subject. 'There were lots of reasons but the appearance was crucial. I don't look anything like him. Our hair has a different texture, our eyes aren't the same. He's an endomorph and I'm an ectomorph. Our characters are different. He's introspective, I'm outgoing. There were plenty of other reasons. Our eyesight's different. He needs glasses for reading; I don't. Our sweat doesn't smell the same. He votes Conservative.'

'Is that relevant?'

'I just threw that one in, but it could be. Conservative fathers nearly always have Conservative sons, ploughing the same furrow. It's all part of the inherited character, staid, safe. But it was when he revealed his bi-sexual side that I began to take a serious interest. Could this man be my father?'

Fascinated now, I asked, 'What did you do?'

My son smiled proudly. 'I organized a DNA test!'

'DNA! DNA!' Marisa said. 'I keep reading it. What does it stand for?'

'The National Dyslexia Association,' I said, and was gratified to see my son smiling at my little joke.

'Deoxyribonucleic acid. It's the most important material of the genes. The DNA molecule is large and complex, but all the information is there. As you can imagine, I spent some time studying the subject. It all began with an Austrian monk called Gregor Mendel in 1865. He practically invented genetics playing around with peas. Peas with round seeds and peas with wrinkled seeds. Amazing what monks get up to but I suppose even they can get bored eventually with praying.'

'So,' I said, 'what did you do?'

'Quite a lot, actually. I had to collect the material from both of us without his knowing. I started with a used handkerchief, then I retrieved a hank of his hair that he had clipped in the bathroom. Next, I stole his toothbrush – do you remember the toothbrush that vanished? – and I even managed to get a sample of his saliva when he spat in the sink.'

Marisa recoiled at the disgusting thoroughness of it. 'My God, you must have been serious,' she said. 'Can you skip the rest?'

'Well I was serious,' he said with a slight smile. 'When I was a little boy you used to tell me "If a job's worth doing, it's worth doing well".'

'Did I really say anything so banal?'

'I'm afraid you did.'

'What happened next?' I asked.

'I bunged all the evidence off to a lab in Cambridge where two of my old friends from Ardingly pursue their esoteric vocations. Their report was unequivocal. It was impossible for Paul to be my father.'

'And you've been walking round with this secret knowledge in your head?' said Marisa. 'I am so sorry, dear.'

'It doesn't matter, Mum. It gave my life a certain *frisson*. I enjoyed myself wondering who my father was. Choosing one, even. I couldn't quite figure out how you had got it together with Sean Connery, but somebody as pretty as you could have pulled anyone you wanted.'

'Hear! Hear!' I said.

'Thank you, gentlemen. Your vote of confidence in my morals is very touching.'

Her son drank a little wine after this exposition – he was not a man, I thought, whose career was going to be damaged by alcohol. The revelations had reduced us all to a thoughtful silence, but we could see that another, larger question floated in the air. Happily Marisa had a less fraught enquiry.

'Apple tart?' she said. 'Or ice cream?'

The men agreed on the more substantial qualities of apple tart, but after she had served us Marisa brought herself an ice cream dripping with chocolate sauce.

'I'm going on a diet,' she said. 'But not today.'

'The funny thing is that when Mother goes on a diet she eats more than I do.'

'That's because I'm eating the correct things. You're not supposed to be hungry when you're on a diet or you want to snack between meals. It's all been worked out by experts.'

'The trouble is,' said Mark, 'there are so many experts.' He looked at his mother, bored with this, and asked, 'Would it be unreasonable to ask who my father is?'

Marisa looked at me with raised eyebrows: the challenge couldn't be ducked.

'I am,' I said. 'Hallo, Son.'

'I *knew* it,' he said. He looked delighted. 'It was when you opened the door. We look alike. We've got the same nose. And then there was the pre-Paul romance that Mum mentioned on the phone. It all fitted in. I have a certain talent for digging up facts, but this didn't require Sherlock Holmes.'

We stood up and embraced and I kissed him on the cheek. I had never kissed a man before. He was all smiles, but I had tears in my eyes which I wiped away quickly.

'I'm sorry it wasn't Sean Connery,' I said.

'I'm not,' he said. 'I'd probably be bald by now.' He released me from a bear-like hug and asked, 'When did *you* know?'

'Very recently. Paul showed me a photograph of himself with you and Samuel. I was stunned.'

'I bet.'

'I'd like to meet Samuel, by the way.'

'You will.'

'I'd like to buy him something. Do boys still play with Meccano and Hornby train sets?'

'I'm afraid not. It's big plastic trucks and cartoon videos these days.'

'What do they learn from that?'

'Nothing. Perhaps you should come round and put him on the right path.'

'I'd enjoy that,' I told him. I missed that sort of thing the first time round but now I had a second chance and could do it properly.

'Well this is one birthday I'll never forget,' said Marisa. There was a euphoric atmosphere around the table. Everybody was smiling. When the plates were empty I produced coffee and we took it into the sitting-room.

'Some questions do arise,' Mark said, when I handed him his cup.

'What are they, dear?' Marisa asked.

He counted questions on his fingers. 'Number one, do we tell Paul? Number two, should I change my name? Number three, how do I tell my wife that she's not actually Mrs Ross? Number four, how do I explain to Samuel that he's the only kid in the world with three grandfathers?'

'I can see that problems have been created as well as solved,' Marisa said. 'But I'm sure we can handle them. Firstly, we don't tell Paul. He couldn't handle it. He's a big enough mess already.'

'Whether you change your name is up to you,' I said. 'I won't be hurt if you don't.'

'It's a good name, Hutton,' he said. 'There was an Edinburgh doctor called James Hutton who founded modern geological theory, and then of course there was Sir Leonard.'

'I don't think Samuel represents a problem,' Marisa said. 'He's too young at the moment to know what a grandfather is.'

'But he calls Paul Grandpa,' said Mark.

Watching Marisa I saw that a small burden of guilt that she

had borne for more than thirty years had been blown away. She seemed to have been refreshed by the day's drama.

'We ought to go out and celebrate,' she said. 'This is a big day for all of us.'

Her son looked glum. 'I wish I could. But there's a small problem at work I have to attend to.'

'You work Sundays?' I asked.

'When don't I work? But you must come round soon to my place so that Susie can meet my father.'

'Susie is your wife?'

'She is. Has she got a shock coming!'

I wondered what Susie, the missing lady in all this, was like. I had acquired a daughter-in-law, too. My bet was that she was bright and probably beautiful.

When Mark had to leave we all stood up. 'It's been wonderful to meet you, Father,' he said. 'You're everything I hoped for.'

There were things I wanted to say but I found myself unable to speak. I smiled and silently embraced him again, dazed at what this year was producing.

AUGUST

Everything stops in August, even the news.
– *Michael Beby*

Friday 6 August

Marisa gave up work today. So now I am naturally worried that she will become bored on her own, or that her life will seem empty. Who knows what little peaks of pleasure or satisfaction were provided by her life in the art gallery?

I took her to the Perkin Warbeck for a celebratory beverage before dinner. It was pleasantly quiet at this early stage of the evening, coping only with the modest requirements of Simon, who owns the garage and drinks exactly two pints of cider every evening, the cravated lecturer (name unknown) whose social life seems to consist of an endless, hopeless quest for company, and the vegetable shop man with his busty squaw.

'This is a nice pub,' Marisa said. 'No noisy yobs demanding attention.'

After months in the lively world of Soho, the virtues of Trebor Avenue's quiet residents guiltily sipping their alcohol must be quite an attraction, but I had other things to talk about.

'Tell me about your parents,' I said.

Tomorrow's trip into the unknown is beginning to weigh on my mind. What were Mr and Mrs Wynn going to make of this new intruder in their daughter's life? When Marisa and I, the teenagers in love, were exhausting each other brainless in the cornfields of Sussex I kept well out of their way. Bonk and bunk was the prevailing rule there. But tomorrow, a mere thirty years after my valiant efforts, I was destined to meet them.

'My dad is a wonderful old gentleman. You'll like him,' said Marisa. 'My mother's a bit highly strung, more verbal, a bit tetchy.'

'What have you told them?'

'That I live with you, obviously. They need an address and phone number for me in case of a crisis. Dad's seventy-nine.'

'What did they say?'

'I didn't give them a chance. I said I'd bring you down to meet them one of these days and we'd explain everything then.'

'They don't connect me with the Mark you knew as a teenager?'

'Not yet, they don't. But I'm going to wise them up.'

'It should be an interesting visit.'

Memo to self: Help!

Saturday 7 August

We drove towards Hardy country in blistering sunshine. We travelled in Marisa's Golf because she knew the way.

Dorchester, with its Roman remains and prehistoric castle, has a bloodthirsty history: the bloody assizes, the Tolpuddle Martyrs. There is even a Roman amphitheatre, the Maumbury Rings, that was the site of well-attended public executions until the eighteenth century. It is now a tourist attraction.

I felt as if I were on trial myself. My judges, Mr and Mrs Wynn, emerged from the large, white front door of their five-bedroom, ivy-covered Regency mansion to embrace their daughter.

'This is Mark,' Marisa said, and we shook hands.

Mrs Wynn was a tall good-looking woman who seemed rather tense. Mr Wynn was a silver-haired character who was now enjoying the leisurely rewards of years of success in the City.

'Call me Joe,' he said to me. Mrs Wynn was less forthcoming with such intimacies. In fact she had difficulty adjusting to the new situation and on a couple of occasions called me Paul.

Indoors, as it was mid-afternoon, we were served tea and cakes in an elegant lounge. The view through the windows was of rolling fields and distant horizons, but in the foreground was a large barn which was part of the property.

'A lovely place to live,' I said admiringly.

'Do you know there are some people round here who have never been to London,' Joe said, and he laughed at the implausibility of it.

'Marisa tells us you own a bookshop?' said Mrs Wynn. I thought she made it sound as if she didn't see much difference between a bookshop and a brothel, but that might have been my paranoia.

'I do,' I told her.

'I must visit it,' said Joe. 'For the first time in my life I've got time to read.'

Marisa seemed happy to delay the revelations she was nursing, and insisted on showing me the garden. I could tell at a glance that its faultless appearance was the work of a professional gardener, and I gathered that such a paragon did indeed come up from the village twice a week to maintain the exquisite condition of the Wynns' acre, in the corner of which were some chickens.

Afterwards I had a shower in the *en suite* bathroom that went with our spacious bedroom, and it wasn't until dinner that the four of us got together again. I approached this meal with some apprehension – the Wynns were going to receive a painful surprise and it was impossible to predict how they were going to react.

The edifice of civilized communication began to crumble when Mrs Wynn looked at the two of us sitting there together and asked: 'How is Paul taking this?'

For Marisa there was now only one way to go.

'Paul is a homosexual,' she said.

'A what?' Mrs Wynn asked, clearly aghast.

'Well he'd tried religion, vegetarianism and teetotalism so I suppose he thought he'd give sodomy a whirl.'

This language appalled her mother. 'Please, Marisa,' she said. 'What are you saying?'

'Paul lives with a man now. Who is homosexual.'

'You poor thing,' said Joe. 'How did it happen?'

'How *do* these things happen?' Marisa said. 'It's a mystery to me.'

Mrs Wynn had recovered sufficiently to ask, 'What does Mark say about it?' She was referring to her grandson, not to me.

'Mark has received a rather large surprise recently,' Marisa said. 'Can I take you both back a few years?'

Her parents stared at her in silence. This was rather more than they had expected when they sat down to dinner (roast lamb with beautiful runner beans).

But Marisa was in full flow – she had been saving this up for thirty years. 'You may remember that when I was seventeen I became pregnant,' she said.

'I remember,' said Mrs Wynn censoriously, and I could see that if you were a pregnant teenager having Mrs Wynn for a mother wouldn't make things any easier.

'But do you remember that I had a boyfriend at that time called Mark?'

'Vaguely,' said Joe, looking puzzled.

'Well it was Mark, not Paul, who was the father of that baby. Mark's father is Mark, not Paul. That's why he's called Mark.'

'This Mark?' asked Joe, looking at me.

'This Mark,' said Marisa. 'He was in love with me then, and he's in love with me now.'

'So why did you marry Paul?' asked Joe, struggling to assimilate the barrage of new information.

'I married him to please Mummy. She didn't want a single mother in the family, if you remember. Mark was in Canada for six months and didn't know that I was pregnant.'

'Oh my God,' cried Mrs Wynn. 'What did we put you through?' She put her hands over her face in an elaborate gesture of contrition.

'You put me through hell frankly, but I've lived through it.'

Joe leaned across and put an arm round his daughter. 'You were very brave, darling. You were a heroine.'

Mrs Wynn, struggling to regain some composure, was wiping her eyes. Her shock was palpable and I feared for her health. But she was soon in control again as a fresh thought alighted in her busy brain. 'At least it provided a father for your baby, and Paul was a good father.'

'But I didn't love him,' Marisa pointed out. 'I was plunged into a nightmare.'

Joe, still with his arm round Marisa, turned to me. Given what he had heard, his attitude towards me must have been ambivalent to say the least, but he managed a propitiatory smile. 'When did you know all about it?' he asked.

'Only this year. I met Paul at a dinner. I didn't even know he had married Marisa. When I got back from Canada you'd moved house.'

'Paul told him where I worked and he came in,' Marisa said. 'It was wonderful. He took me out to dinner.'

'And Mark knows?'

'He knew already. He'd done some DNA tests and found out that Paul wasn't his father. I only discovered that a couple of weeks ago.'

'How extraordinary,' said Joe. 'And he's all right about it?'

'He's rather pleased, actually,' Marisa told him.

A strange silence fell on the table as our hosts digested the traumatic news. My interpretation was that Mrs Wynn was wrestling with feelings of guilt, while her husband was just confused as he tried to put the pieces of the jigsaw into place.

'What's going to happen now?' he asked.

'Mark and I are going to get married,' Marisa said. 'Better late than never.'

Memo to self: A new wife, a son, a grandson, a daughter-in-law, two new in-laws. I'm collecting relatives like a tegestologist collects beermats.

Sunday 8 August

I woke up feeling surprisingly chirpy and went to the window to admire the Dorset landscape. Marisa was still in the deepest of sleeps and I wasn't going to wake her up. Beneath the window, Joe, in a Ralph Lauren dressing-gown, was collecting eggs from his chickens. This routine was such a novelty to me that I got dressed and went down to join him.

'Good morning,' I said. 'We get ours from Tesco.'

'Not eggs like this, you don't,' he said. 'How are you, Mark? That was some story we heard last night.'

'You had to be told it,' I said, 'but I hope it didn't disturb your sleep.'

He reached for another brown egg from the henhouse. 'I did stay awake a bit,' he admitted. 'It was a lot to take in.'

'How's Helen?' I asked. It seemed all right to use her name to him, even if I hadn't been invited to use it to her.

'She's been a bit tearful, to tell you the truth, wondering where she went wrong in 1972.'

'She mustn't reproach herself,' I said gallantly. 'It's how people behaved at that time.'

When Marisa eventually surfaced we had fresh eggs for breakfast, a treat that made me decide that one day I must have my own chickens.

'I thought I'd take you out today,' Marisa said to me, 'and introduce you to the restorative powers of West Country air. How about Lyme Regis?'

And so after breakfast we got in the Golf and headed west across south Dorset. The place names in this favoured corner of England were unusual and often double-barrelled: Winterbourne Steepleton, Burton Bradstock, Whitchurch Canonicorum, Wynford Eagle.

Lyme Regis was one of the first seaside resorts in the south-west, assiduously promoted by Jane Austen. Its main street slopes down to a wide, hill-cliffed bay. We walked along the front to the old harbour, called the Cobb. It was famous from a scene in the film *The French Lieutenant's Woman*, but I never saw the film. While we were sitting on the Cobb we came to a momentous decision.

'I've been thinking,' Marisa said, 'about the fact that I no longer earn any money.'

'I hope that isn't going to worry you,' I replied. 'My God, Mrs Pringle is selling books even as we sit here!'

Marisa didn't seem impressed by this news. 'Can I ask you a question?' she said.

'You don't need permission.'

'You might resent it. It's none of my business.'

'My business is your business, kid. You've got to pretend that we're already married.'

'OK,' she said. 'Here goes. How much money do you make every week out of the bookshop?'

'Obviously it varies. There are good weeks and bad weeks. Also, it's seasonal. I sell ten times as many books in December as I do in February.'

'But averaging it out?'

'Well, forgetting the Christmas rush, I suppose it's about five hundred in a good week and nearer four hundred in a bad one.' The figures embarrassed me and I hurried to explain: 'But I own the shop and the flat and so have no expenses like rent or mortgage.'

'And you work six full days a week.'

'Unless I'm chasing some lady in an art gallery.'

'But Mark,' she said, 'you're sitting on a fortune.'

'You make me sound like a whore.'

'You could make several hundred pounds a week without getting out of bed.'

'Now you make me sound like a gigolo.'

'You've got sex on the brain.'

'And only sex will get it off.'

'Well we can't do anything about that here. Listen, you could sell the shop to one of the big chains who are expanding everywhere for half a million, and invest the money in Jersey or somewhere where you'll get ten per cent.'

'Half a million? I don't think I'd get that.'

'Not for the shop alone. But Mrs Pringle is leaving, and one of the big boys would convert the flat into a second floor for the shop. It would be quite big and it's in an excellent position. You ought to think about it.'

'I'm thinking,' I said. It had never occurred to me to sell the shop. For some reason I felt tied to it. But the dramatic change the sale would bring to the rest of my life made it an exciting idea.

'And there's another thing,' Marisa said. 'If you sold the shop, you could sell the house. You wouldn't need to be in Trebor Avenue any more.'

'I see a snag,' I said. 'Where would I live? I've got used to living indoors.'

'You'd buy a lovely place in the country, a cottage with roses over the door.'

'Would I be able to see haystacks?'

'Very likely. What do you think? You invest the shop money, and use the house money to buy a cottage. Then you live on the interest from the invested money.'

'What do I think? I'm living with you in a beautiful cottage in the country and don't have to go to work? It's a difficult call.'

'Don't rush into it.'

'Where do these financial insights come from?' I asked. 'Inherited from your father?'

'It must be in the genes. As a girl I used to visit Daddy in his office, and got quite attracted to the high-flown financial chatter that drifted round his mahogany desk. It's a world where money breeds money. Daddy always hoped I would join him for a highly rewarded, hard-nosed life in one of those huge buildings but, as you know, pregnancy intervened.'

I stood up to look at the sea where several small sailing boats were chasing each other, perhaps in a race. Apparently the first skirmish between Drake's fleet and the Armada took place in this bay.

'What are you going to do?' Marisa asked.

I pointed at a coffee shop up the road. 'I'm going to take you up there for a coffee,' I said. 'And then I'm going to sell the shop.'

Monday 9 August

Protocol dictated that I returned the Wynns' hospitality by taking them out to dinner and they directed us towards the King's Arms in Dorchester. It is a hotel with a crowded history, having been dispensing sherbet for hundreds of years, initially as a sort of staging post between London and Exeter. Its past customers include George III, Queen Victoria, Lord Nelson, Thomas Hardy, who could be spotted scribbling plots in the upstairs bay window while enjoying morning coffee, Lawrence of Arabia, Augustus John and Pavlova who was in the area to study the swans at Abbotsbury before producing her most famous ballet performance in *The Dying Swan*.

I was in a buoyant mood after the Lyme Regis decision; Marisa had lifted a weight off my back. The bottle of red wine I was sharing with Joe disappeared very quickly and we had to order another. Mrs Wynn's disapproval of this rapid consumption drew an impressive reply from her husband who was taking advantage of the freedom offered tonight.

'It's good for you, darling,' he said, and before she could contradict he swept on, assisted by the stimulation of the product he was defending. 'The antioxidants in red wine help prevent blood clotting and the build-up of cholesterol. Look at the French. They eat twice as much fat as us and they smoke more, but they have half as many heart attacks as we do. Why? Because they drink red wine like we drink tea.'

'You can always think of a good reason,' said Mrs Wynn, 'for doing something naughty.'

'It's a talent that has served me well over the years,' said Joe. 'Now when's this marriage?' He turned to Marisa and me, perhaps to escape a tart reply from his wife.

'As soon as possible,' I told him. 'But there are a few amenities to observe first.'

'Like divorce,' said Marisa. 'Why? Are you coming to this wedding?' She turned to me. 'Daddy wasn't there when I married Paul.'

'I was in Washington,' Joe protested. 'The wedding was too sudden for me to get back. That's why I'm looking forward to this one. My daughter the bride!'

'You won't miss this one,' I promised.

'Where would it take place?' Mrs Wynn asked Marisa. Arousing her enthusiasm was going to be a more demanding exercise.

'I don't like that "would" much,' Marisa told her. 'You mean "will". And you can get married anywhere these days, can't you? How about in a pub?'

Mrs Wynn looked horrified at this suggestion. 'What do you say, Mark?' she asked.

'I've waited thirty years to marry her,' I said. 'I'm hardly likely to start arguing about the venue.'

'I think a nice quiet wedding in a register office would be best,' said Joe.

'I expect that's what it will be, Dad,' Marisa told him.

When we went into the lounge for a coffee his mind had moved on to the subject of wedding presents. He anticipated fewer guests than would be found at most weddings, and consequently fewer gifts. This worried him and he said he would make up for it.

I was thinking about a cottage in the country that would

require furnishing. There would be plenty of opportunity, I thought, for my new father-in-law to show his generosity.

Tuesday 10 August

We arrived home to be greeted by sensational news. Charles Westacott has been arrested! It happened yesterday apparently, but Dorset was a news-free zone. The arrest took place by arrangement in his solicitor's office in London. Charles was charged with stealing just over a million pounds from one of the firms where he is a director. He is alleged to have diverted the cash to an off-shore account in the Channel Isles.

His picture is in all the papers, a happy smiling photograph that was obviously taken before yesterday's events. One report refers to a garden party he threw last month which cost £150,000. The implication that in the normal course of events he would not be able to afford such extravagance is clear enough, but legal restrictions prevented the paper from spelling this out.

He made a brief appearance in court yesterday afternoon and was remanded on bail until next month. I can't begin to imagine how Janet is reacting. Was she ever curious about where all the money was coming from? Perhaps she didn't know quite how much there was, quietly fructifying in Jersey or Guernsey.

I remember describing him back in January as being like a man with seven watches up his sleeve so there has to be something dodgy about him. And Rupert Barkley must have had his suspicions when he expressed surprise at the lavishness of the party last month.

But recently I have started to like him. He may have become

a lord, but he didn't lord it over me. I liked the way he didn't take himself too seriously at his party. He has also, of course, been very generous and I haven't been slow to accept his hospitality. The fact that it now looks as if he was being generous with someone else's money doesn't detract from the fact that he was spending it on me.

Friday 20 August

I went to church today. Nothing could surprise me more than that simple declarative sentence except perhaps the reason I went there.

It began, as things seem to have done this year, with a phone call from Luke.

'They're holding a memorial service for Arnold Thacker on Friday,' he said. 'I think we ought to go.'

'What on earth for?' I asked.

'Public relations. Anyway, I've been thinking. Perhaps we were too harsh on the old sod. We blamed him for our failures, but was it his fault? Paul didn't become a vet because he had a pregnant teenage wife and needed to earn money. Andrew made a bundle before he lost it. I'm quite well off and you've got your own business. Is it Thacker's fault that Jamie Croft preferred the bright lights? What do we blame Thacker for?'

'He beat the hell out of us, Luke, for no good reason. Brown got flogged for farting.'

'Teachers did that in those days. Anyway, I'll feel better if I show up at his service.'

'OK,' I said reluctantly.

Mrs Pringle deputized for the last time and I drove to the church which was very near my old school. Surprisingly it was more than half full, but when I looked around for faces from my past I saw that the congregation consisted of more recent pupils, no doubt creepers and toadies, who were unknown to me.

Paul and Andrew had succumbed to Luke's blandishments and sat together at the back with identical po-faced expressions. I couldn't see whether they were holding hands.

The rector recited a couple of prayers, the congregation sang a hymn I didn't know, and then Mr Young, the present headmaster at our old alma mater and Thacker's last boss, delivered what I suppose is called a eulogy. By the time Young had finished, Thacker sounded like Mr Chips.

'Today we honour the memory of a kind and considerate teacher who devoted his life to improving the minds of a younger generation,' he began.

'Can you shout "Bollocks" in church?' I asked Luke.

'They don't encourage it.'

Hearing us talk, Mr Young threw an understanding smile in our direction, evidently believing that we were fondly recalling a kind moment from Thacker's compassionate career.

'He was a revered teacher who put his pupils first,' he said, having obviously forgotten the occasion when he had to suspend Thacker for beating a pupil. He was like a modern politician, pouring lies in your face and thinking that you believed him. How have we allowed these people to arrive at the conclusion that we're simple? I became so angry that I was on the verge of making a discreet intervention, but he suddenly changed tack.

'Today we are launching an appeal for a fund that will commemorate Arnold Thacker's sterling qualities. It will be called the Arnold Thacker Scholarship. Why does a free school need a scholarship? you may ask. Today there are boys from poorer homes who have the ability to go to Oxford or

Cambridge but can't afford it without incurring hideous debts. The Arnold Thacker Scholarship will send the poorest boy to Oxbridge at no expense at all. There is a table at the back of the church where you can make your contributions and commitments as you leave. I hope you will be generous. Arnold Thacker deserves no less.'

We found Paul and Andrew queuing at the table. Andrew was holding five twenty-pound notes, Paul was writing a cheque.

'A hundred quid then?' said Luke.

'I think so,' said Paul.

I surprised everyone by producing ten ten pound notes. I had taken to carrying a fuller wallet since Colin Newman increased my overdraft limit.

'But you didn't like Thacker,' said Luke.

'I know a good cause when I see one,' I said.

'I think we'll all feel better for this,' said Paul in his holiest voice.

Thursday 26 August

Mrs Pringle left today. Removal men spent half the morning carting her stuff downstairs, while she sat in the shop and said how much she would miss it. I think she has become a little worried about how she will get on with her sister when they're living cheek by jowl.

Marisa came in with a splendid piece of jewellery – a necklace, I think – that she had bought and we gave it to Mrs Pringle as a farewell present. I wanted to open a bottle of something, but she doesn't drink.

At midday her taxi arrived to sweep her off to the seaside. We stood outside to wave her off.

Afterwards we went up to her flat.

'It's huge,' said Marisa. 'It could be turned into the second floor of a shop quite easily.'

'Let the sale proceed,' I said.

SEPTEMBER

In September you have to fly to Spain
to keep the summer going.
– Huw Thomas

Monday 6 September

I reached work early this morning to do a special job. It is Phoebe's publication day and I had to change the window for it. Her publishers had sent me a very flattering picture of her which bore the tag LOCAL AUTHOR, and this was the centre of my display.

I had been persuaded to increase the order from four dozen to six dozen, partly by an importunate salesman, and partly by the news of the film deal. Now I had to sell them – seventy-two copies at £17 less a penny is £1,274 worth of books and I was keen to find the buyers. The window display was intended to lure and persuade.

In the first hour I sold five copies which was very encouraging. I asked one of the customers if she knew Phoebe, expecting her to be supporting a friend. But she said she didn't and had bought the book because she was impressed by the reviews. I didn't know there had been any reviews.

The book has a pale-blue cover with the title and author's name in ornate gold. It looks very dignified. The paperback, when it appears next year, will probably feature a wheelie bin with a leg sticking out.

At eleven o'clock the progenitor of this masterpiece arrived in what looked like a green boiler suit. It seemed unlikely that she had come in for a quick chat about post-structuralism.

'I thought I'd sign all your copies,' she said.

'That's a very good idea,' I told her, and began to collect

them and carry them to my desk. Phoebe sat down and happily scribbled her signature in all of them. She handed the last one to me.

'I'll pay for that. I've signed it to you.'

'That's very kind of you,' I said, surprised.

'You encouraged me on New Year's Eve by saying it sounded promising. I know I was drunk, but you were the first person to take me seriously.'

I took the copy and opened it to read the first sentence: *When Maggie was five years old she was given a puppy*. I was not sure that this sounded like my sort of novel but I was touched by her gesture.

'I'd wish you luck with it,' I said, 'but you don't need luck. You've already done bloody well with the film deal.'

She stood up and then sat on the desk. 'Have you seen any reviews?' she asked diffidently.

'Not yet,' I admitted.

She pulled some press cuttings from her pocket. 'I just happen to have a few here,' she said with a smile.

I took all the books back and attached a SIGNED BY THE AUTHOR label to each. Then I went to my desk and sat down to read Phoebe's reviews while she watched me. They were unanimously in favour:

'A glorious look at the turbulent world of matrimony with incisive insights about why it so often fails' – *Daily Mail*.

'At a deeper level the novel is a metaphor about the perils of human relationships and the attendant hazards of the search for love' – *Observer*.

'Laugh your socks off when the sex war comes to the kitchen' – *Sun*.

'Maggie Radford turns herself into a sociological palimpsest, the legible subtext of which is fascinating because of her heroic denial of her true character' – *Guardian*.

'Audacious, accurate, argumentative' – *Daily Telegraph.*

'You must be very happy with these,' I said.

'There was a nasty one by a misogynist in the *Express*, headed "Feeble Phoebe" but I didn't bring that one in.' She pointed towards the shop. 'You have customers.'

There were three people, each holding a copy of Phoebe's novel.

'Friends of yours?' I asked.

'Never seen them before.'

'Blimey,' I said, 'you've got a hit on your hands.'

Wednesday 8 September

Marisa has taken over responsibility for selling the shop. She was keen to do it, and I suspect that she has a better commercial head than I have. She will deal with the agents and potential buyers, while I quietly dismantle my little empire. It has become depressingly clear that quite a lot of work is involved – I've got to contact publishers, settle accounts, get rid of the books, and then deal with electricity people, telephone people, insurance people and council people.

Marisa phoned a commercial agent she had known in Soho and, with the scent of commission in his nostrils, he was in the shop within an hour. He was about thirty with blond hair parted in the middle, and he seldom stopped moving. He paid three visits to the flat upstairs. His equipment included an expensive camera, a recording machine housed in his pocket into which he chatted from time to time, and one of those modern replacements for the tape measure, a Leica laser meter which used rays to tell you the length of a room without you moving. There was also a large red notebook into which he copied details of the shop's recent accounts.

'Busy town, prime site, lots of room,' he said, either to us or his recording machine. 'Selling candy to babies.'

'Does that mean you think you'll find a buyer?' Marisa asked.

'No problem, darling.' This time he was talking to her.

'How soon?'

'Ah,' he said. 'Sometimes these things aren't that quick. You get the fish on the hook, but the fish has to take a lot of things into account.'

'How many fish are there?' Marisa asked.

'Six.'

'That ought to be enough,' she said calmly.

Memo to self: Thank God she's handling it. That blond ponce would drive me nuts.

Sunday 12 September

I met Samuel today. He's a very bright two year old who never stops smiling. A family conference decided that he would call me Mark.

His mother Susie is a slim and attractive blonde of twenty-nine who is the coolly efficient wife that Mark needs. I expect he had a large field to choose from.

They had invited us to Sunday lunch. Now that Mrs Pringle has disappeared into the wild blue yonder, no other day is available to me. They live in a town house not far from Mark's hospital, and Samuel has a playroom to himself. I ventured into this alien territory and discovered a floor strewn with toys, including a trampoline and a car that he can sit in. Samuel offered me various other toys and told me what they were called and what they could do. His conversation was excellent, but later over lunch when I was discussing the shop sale he felt excluded and became irritable. 'What's Mark torting about?' he demanded.

Susie, of course, was fascinated by me, her husband's mysterious father. She gave me all the best food.

'It's a bit late in the day to meet your father-in-law,' she said. 'I've got some catching up to do.' She had a low provocative voice that she could have sold to an advertising agency.

'It's a relief to find that my son has the same excellent taste as his father,' I replied, congratulating myself on the neat way I had managed to compliment both women in the room at the same time.

'I'm so glad you're Mark's real father,' she said. 'I was always afraid he might grow to become like Paul. Men do things like that without even noticing.' She had a flirtatious way with her that I found quite captivating. She wasn't the remote figure I thought I was seeing when we were introduced.

'Which aspect of Paul did you not want him to emulate?' I asked out of curiosity. 'Apart from the sex thing, of course.'

'The extremist tendency,' she answered promptly. 'No alcohol, no meat, the religion business. Paul can't see a cause without embracing it totally. I see that as a weakness. I want a bit more scrutiny, some reservations, deeper judgements.'

'Brainy as well as beautiful, your wife,' I said to Mark. 'Where did you find her?'

Marisa answered for him. 'They met on a weekend course at Oxford. Susie was studying psychology. Two brain boxes together. He rang me that night to say "I've found my wife".'

'And you said "I didn't know you'd lost one".' He turned to me. 'Just watching her draw a chart released a flood of endorphins in my brain, so I invited her out for a glass of bitter.'

'It was odd actually,' Susie said, 'because I love bitter and nobody had ever offered me one before.'

'She thought I had extraordinary powers of perception. The truth was that I was broke and a half of bitter was the cheapest thing on offer.'

'Daddy was broke,' said Samuel, hugely amused. We decided that he was thinking about a toy that broke.

Mark started to refill our wine glasses. I didn't recognize a single label and assumed they were more expensive brands than I am used to. He wouldn't be worrying about the price of a half of bitter today.

'I went to see Paul last week,' he told us when he had filled the glasses.

'What for?' Marisa asked uneasily.

'I thought I should. He was my father for a long time. At least he thought he was.'

'How is he?' I asked.

'He's got financial problems. I gave him some money.'

'Not too much, I hope,' said Susie.

'He spent enough on me over the years. But now he's probably missing Mum's contribution from the art gallery.'

'He should have thought of that when he invited Andrew in,' Marisa said. 'What does Andrew earn?'

'Nothing,' said Mark. 'He's got this idea of the two of them starting a taxi business. All the popular destinations are within thirty miles – Heathrow, Gatwick, the Channel Tunnel, London, Brighton. The only snag is that Andrew has lost his driving licence.'

'A slight drawback,' I said.

'You didn't tell him anything, did you?' asked Marisa.

'God, no. And I never will. He looks pretty fragile already.'

'Perhaps his new lifestyle isn't suiting him,' I said.

'He asked after you, Mum. He asked whether Mark was looking after you properly.'

'What do you mean – fragile?' Marisa asked.

'He's lost a bit of weight. Probably he's not eating enough now that you're not there to cook for him.'

'Or?'

'There are more than thirty sexually transmitted diseases today compared with two in 1960. And there are certain illnesses that seem to be associated with the life he's chosen. We can all think of half-a-dozen famous ones who didn't reach fifty.'

Marisa didn't like this. 'Don't talk like that,' she said. 'He hasn't been doing it all his life.'

'No, you're quite right,' he said apologetically. 'It's just that he doesn't look well.'

Samuel piped up in the silence that followed this discussion. 'Where's Grandpa Ross?' he asked.

'At his house,' said Susie. 'Perhaps we should have him round for dinner. Fatten him up and please Samuel.'

'He wouldn't come without Andrew, and I'm not having him here,' said Mark firmly.

The conversation seemed to have depressed Marisa and I took her hand and told her to cheer up. She ignored this and turned to Mark.

'I don't suppose you got around to the subject of divorce?'

Mark shook his head. 'I'm afraid I didn't. It's not really my business, is it?'

'The trouble is,' said Marisa, 'it's not his business either. What does he need a divorce for?'

Wednesday 15 September

Bow Street magistrates have sent Charles Westacott for a November trial at the Old Bailey. It was on the news tonight, complete with shots of Charles leaving court with his solicitor and waving, somewhat inappropriately, at the waiting cameras. It was a brave show because it does not look good.

There are five counts of obtaining a money transfer by deception and using false instruments which means forging cheques. The attitude of the law towards this sort of thing has always seemed lopsided to me. You can beat someone up in the street and get off with a warning, but if you steal money from a large corporation they lock you up because it undermines the system. Property has always been more important than people in the country's courtrooms. It dates back to the landowners of the seventeenth century.

So Charles is heading for a spell in the choky but behaves as if he doesn't think he is. Interestingly, the television footage showed no sign of Janet, standing by her man. Perhaps she was having a massage.

Reporting restrictions weren't lifted so the accounts in tomorrow's papers will be brief. But the downfall of a politician is always popular with the Press so I expect the size of the picture will make up for it.

Monday 20 September

As usual when I got home from the shop I switched on Ceefax to see what had been going on in the world while I wasn't looking. Had the Queen abdicated, or the Prime Minister resigned?

The item that caught my attention concerned the Booker Prize. The shortlist had been announced and I dutifully punched up the relevant page. The finalists were Martin Amis and Beryl Bainbridge, of course, followed by an austere Canadian spinster who had produced a sombre novel about witchcraft in Salem, and a South African academic, better known for his poetry, whose bleak novel about two races trying to live together had been widely praised. Number five was a young Indian novelist who despite living in Calcutta had a literary equivalent of Delhi belly: his verbal diarrhoea invariably produced novels of 900 pages which took precious shelf space from two other writers. And the sixth candidate? Phoebe Davenport for her debut novel, *How To Bin Your Husband.*

I nearly fell out of my chair.

It couldn't be avoided any longer. I would have to read the book. I found the copy that Phoebe had signed for me and opened it with a certain curiosity.

> When Maggie was five years old she was given a puppy. It was run over by a boy in a van. The grief Maggie suffered changed her personality for ever.

Actually I wanted to read on now.

Marisa came in from the kitchen where she had been grilling steaks, and I held the book up. 'Shortlisted for the Booker Prize,' I told her.

'I'm not surprised,' she said. 'I've read it. It's brilliant.'

'I was afraid it might be,' I said.

Thursday 30 September

Potential buyers have been traipsing through the shop. Sometimes they don't introduce themselves but just come in to spy. The more serious ones have to reveal their identity because they want to look at the flat upstairs.

Marisa, initially encouraged by the optimism of her blond-headed agent, had become depressed at the absence of offers.

She was about to ring him when he walked into the shop this afternoon with a complacent smile on his face. Luckily Maria was there at the time, studying the mysteries of bookselling.

'The fish is on the hook,' he announced.

'It took a long time,' she complained.

'I talked to a lot of fishes,' he told her with a sly grin. 'I've contacted every major bookshop chain and I think I've found a gap in their market. Some of them have been down here to have a look.'

'I noticed,' I said.

He glanced round at the shop. 'I've put the price up, by the way.'

'Up?' said Marisa. 'To what?'

'Seven hundred and fifty.'

I liked the sound of the price hike, but thought it was too hopeful. And yet, I wondered, who knew nowadays? Prices would suddenly move upwards with no explanation and then, just as suddenly, they would drop again. Perhaps we had chosen a month when they were going up.

'Seven hundred and fifty gives them some leeway,' the agent explained. 'They'll always want to knock a bit off for the sake of their pride.'

'I'm sure we'd be very happy with seven hundred,' said Marisa. 'Who's on the hook?'

'A chain that stretches from Plymouth to Inverness. They're a firm in a hurry – targets to meet, competitors to crush. I wouldn't be surprised if they paid the full price.'

Memo to self: I would.

OCTOBER

It's a funny kind of month, October. For the really keen cricket fan it's when you discover that your wife left you in May.

– *Denis Norden*

Thursday 7 October

I had to stay up late this evening to watch the by-election result. They've been voting all day in the grimy northern constituency where Charles Westacott once reigned, trying to choose his successor. It is one of the safest Labour seats in the country, but the word from the opinion pollsters was that the result could be a shock.

And sure enough, soon after midnight, we were treated to the delicious spectacle of tormented politicians, struggling to accept the public's unexpected verdict. LIB DEM GAIN flashed across the screen even as the result was being announced, and the hard-looking man who thought that he would be slipping into Charles's seat in the House of Commons glowered at the pretty young lady who would, as if throttling her was an option he was still considering.

The studio pundits, hired to explain this political earthquake, looked as baffled as he did. The Labour majority that Charles had received at the last election was over 25,000. The Liberal Democrats had taken the seat with a majority of just under 700.

Each pundit had a different explanation for this seismic shift. One thought it was 'mid-term blues' which hit every government. The second thought that the manner in which Charles had turned his back on the constituency and sauntered off to the House of Lords had not gone down well with loyal Labour voters, but the third raised the subject of Charles's appearance at Bow Street Magistrates' Court, carefully skating through *sub judice* territory to suggest that the local Labour activists were fighting with one hand tied behind their backs.

The pretty young lady made a graceful speech in which she promised that the days of 'spin and sleaze' were over. It is usual for new MPs to pay a compliment to their predecessors in a maiden speech in the Commons. I wonder what she will find to say about Charles?

Friday 8 October

Janet Westacott rang me this evening. This wasn't the forthright, confident woman I used to know, but a new shyer version from whom all assurance had drained.

'I wondered if you could do me a favour,' she asked in subdued tones.

'Of course.'

'Come round and talk to Charles.'

The request surprised me. Charles and I were hardly close.

'Why me?' I asked.

'Charles likes you. He hasn't got many friends left, Mark, and the by-election result hasn't helped. He'd love to see you and have a talk.'

'OK,' I said.

He was sitting on a rattan chair in his conservatory, staring at nothing in particular and wearing a pair of old corduroys and a knitted blue sweater.

'Mark's come to see you,' Janet said.

He came alive and jumped to his feet. 'That's kind of you, Mark. It's good to see you. What'll you drink?'

'Have you got any of that sloe gin left?' I asked, feeling a little awkward. (Did he know that Janet had asked me to come?) When we sat down with our drinks he lit a large cigar, obviously taking his pleasures while he still could. His drink was an Islay malt whisky.

'You followed it all?' he asked.

'I saw your picture in the paper,' I told him.

'The day I left school my headmaster said I'd either end up in the House of Lords or in prison. He never dreamt it would be both.'

'Well, hang on. You haven't been convicted yet,' I said, in a fatuous attempt to raise his spirits.

'But I think we all know which way it's going.'

'And it'll be prison?'

'It's unavoidable, I'm told. The only question is for how long?' He puffed on his cigar and gave me a long look. 'I expect you wonder why I did it?'

'It does cross one's mind,' I admitted.

He nodded as if this was a problem that had to be addressed. 'My father hanged himself. Did you know that?' I shook my head. 'We had no money when I was a kid. My father was in and out of work and he had four children to bring up. My mother was worn out by the effort of it, but it was the constant money shortage that ground them both down. Our food was the cheapest, our clothes were the oldest, the gas was always being cut off and we were the only family in the street without a television. How other people got money, sometimes lots of money, remained a mystery in the Westacott household. I did a paper round for four shillings a week. Some weeks it was the only money that came into the house. My father was an excellent carpenter but work was almost impossible to find. And then one day, destroyed by it all, he hanged himself in his shed. I joined the Labour Party the following week.' He paused to drink some whisky. 'This doesn't explain anything of course, still less excuse it. I'm just giving you the background.'

'How old are you, Charles?' I asked. I knew that Janet was forty.

'Forty-five. After twenty years in the Labour Party I became an MP. I'd seen enough to want to do something for the poor, but thinking constantly about money I became obsessed with it. It's at the bottom of every problem. People don't get enough of it. You've got one short life on this planet and you're supposed to spend it counting pennies, begging for loans, scraping along and denying yourself even quite ordinary things like foreign holidays. For every cheque in the post there are ten bills and the demand never stops. You must find that yourself?'

'I do,' I said. 'I've never earned enough money.'

'You've got an old car, a small house, you never seem to have a holiday, and you've been working all your life.'

'I think that sums it up,' I said.

'Well MPs don't get paid much by the standards that prevail elsewhere, and they have a lot of expenses over and above the official allowance. They used to say that every Prime Minister leaves Downing Street with an overdraft. That's why they all rush to write their memoirs. The whole thing's a nightmare unless you have other incomes.'

'So you nicked a million quid?' I said boldly.

He didn't flinch. 'So they say. It was too easy. Just bits of paper travelling across my desk. Could an MP afford a house like this one? Could he give a party like the one I had in July? Could he dress his wife in the stuff that Janet wears? What's he supposed to do?'

A few answers that didn't involve stealing a million occurred to me, but I hadn't come here to censure. He was having a bad enough time without my contribution, and he didn't look well.

'Didn't all those boards you sat on produce lots of money?' I asked.

'Not lots, no. Free dinners, free tickets to the theatre, free air tickets sometimes, but part-time directorships don't produce very fat fees. Not in my case, anyway. I think I was supposed to feel honoured to be on the team.'

He noticed my glass was empty and filled it up.

'Well, if you *do* go to prison,' I said, trying to make it sound as if this was an unlikely development, 'if there's anything I can do ...'

'Thanks,' he said. 'You could keep an eye on Janet. You know, keep in touch with her.'

'How's she taking it?'

'Very badly. It wasn't something she could ever have anticipated. Her life has been turned upside down. She isn't who she thought she was. It's bloody awful.' For the first time he looked genuinely distraught, but struggled to recover as Janet appeared.

'Are you boys having a nice chat?' she asked with a brave gaiety.

'We're covering the ground,' said Charles. 'Drink?'

'I think I'll have one of what Mark's drinking.'

'Have you heard from Emma?' I asked, as Charles poured a sloe gin. I knew that Emma wouldn't be one of the friends who had deserted her.

'She sent us an invitation to her film premiere from America.'

'America?'

'They're about to film Phoebe's book. I think they've Americanized it to maximize the audience.'

'Oh dear,' I said. 'Phoebe will love that.'

'She's got her money,' said Janet. 'She's a lucky girl.' I realized that she was adapting to her new situation very quickly, already accepting that she was now the one with no money. 'The premiere's in London next month, but obviously we won't be going. Rupert and Emma are flying over for the big night. I'd love to be there.'

Suddenly she burst into tears. Charles was out of his chair like a shot to embrace her.

'Come on, dear,' he said. 'We've got to get through this.'

'I know,' she muttered, pressing her face to his chest.

I was embarrassed and felt like an intruder. I stood up. 'I think I must be off,' I said. 'I'll let myself out.' They didn't reply and I moved towards the door. 'Good luck, Charles,' I said.

I left them then, locked in a tearful embrace. I don't think they noticed me go.

Monday 18 October

The news arrived today. The shop is sold. Our brilliant agent, the man with the attractive blond hair and engaging manner, came in to deliver the news himself. The buyers have agreed to pay £700,000 on one condition – that we are out in a fortnight, by 1 November. They want to open their new-look shop a month later to catch the Christmas trade.

This is perfectly understandable, but has put a little pressure on me. I spent the morning clearing my voluminous desk and was surprised at the stuff I found in it.

Brochures for seminars that I should have attended: Successful Marketing for the Small Bookshop; Maximizing Sales & Profits of Non-Book Products in Bookshops; Making Your Shop Front Work for You.

There were the dozens of verses I had scribbled in moments of boredom. Letters from Luke in Australia, written when we didn't expect to meet again. Maps of places I hoped to visit. First editions of newspapers that have since died. Invitations to weddings that I probably didn't attend. Press cuttings about events that seemed sensational at the time. Letters from former girlfriends that made me sad. Photographs that never reached an album. Wimbledon programmes, theatre programmes, keep-fit programmes. Author interviews, ripped from magazines. Letters from the bank, mostly impatient. Advertisements for Mark Hutton Books that had appeared in different local papers over the years.

It was with a wonderful feeling of release that I discovered I could consign the lot into the empty black plastic sacks that sat, mouth open, at my feet.

The next problem was: What do I do with all these books? It would have taken several hours and a pocket calculator to work out the value of the volumes that perched unsold on my shelves, and I had hoped that the buyer of the shop would buy them – stock at valuation, it's called. But they have their own safe choice of books already waiting in several gigantic warehouses, and didn't want mine.

Tuesday 19 October

We managed to combine cuddles and culture this evening. Comfortably curled up on the sofa we watched the live coverage of the Booker prizegiving. It involved a dinner at the Guildhall where among about 500 guests were the six nervous finalists. The programme was padded out with interviews with the authors, filmed earlier, and the knowing chat of literary luminaries in the studio, striving to pick the winner while the guests munched their way through three courses.

We could see Phoebe sitting at a large table with her publisher and various guests. Having no agent or family there was nobody she could ask along, but she looked quite happy with the alcohol that surrounded her. I was worried that, if she won, her acceptance speech would verge on the incoherent, but at least for once she had put on a decent dress. In contrast to her competitors she seemed cheerful and laughed a lot, surprised to be there. The other finalists looked solemn, ruthlessly ambitious and quite prepared to slash their wrists if the judges made a silly mistake.

I had finally read the book and could see why it had reached this exalted shortlist. In her bilious portrayal of the male sex she had managed to maintain a proper balance. Maggie Radford, having learned to hate men from an early age, was nevertheless a sexually normal woman who wanted children and believed they needed a father. In the end she had three husbands but no children which only strengthened her belief in men's uselessness. The men Phoebe described were decent enough; she cleverly resisted the temptation to demonize them. But the venomous treatment they received from Maggie lifted the book to furious and sometimes hilarious heights. The typical male reader, I thought, wouldn't know whether to laugh or hide.

The book had waltzed off the shelf in my shop. Forty of the sixty copies went in a fortnight, and the rest disappeared in the wake of the Booker selection. In normal circumstances it would have been the moment to reorder, but as I am selling the shop I didn't.

In an interview that seemed to have been filmed beside the Thames, Phoebe was invited by her earnest young interrogator to explain her apparent hostility to men. She replied with a charm I had not seen before that some of her best friends were men, but 'a certain parity' had to be restored after centuries of male domination.

'She's very good,' said Marisa.

'She is,' I agreed, 'but don't become a disciple.'

None of the studio pundits thought she would win, although they voted for women. They were split between Beryl Bainbridge and the lady from Canada who sat poker-faced at her table in a strange dress rimmed by Canadian fur. But one female critic in the studio described Phoebe's book as 'a brave foray on behalf of women' and thought that she would probably take the prize one day. The man on her left, a reviewer in one of the weeklies, said the book frightened him.

When the eating in the hall had finished and television time was running out, the chairman of the judges, a former Cabinet minister whose high-flying career had been cruelly truncated when he was caught bonking a topless model in Hyde Park, rose to deliver the judges' verdict. He provided a lucid precis of each of the contenders' efforts, and contrived in some way to praise them all.

'But the prize this year,' he said, 'for his gripping picture of strife in Kashmir, goes to Rahul Khanna and *Himalayan Journey*.'

'Well,' said Marisa.

'You couldn't expect her to win,' I said. 'She did bloody well to get this far.'

'I'm fed up now.'

'Well she doesn't seem to be.' A shot appeared on the screen of Phoebe applauding the winner and laughing gaily. She was surrounded by empty wine bottles.

NOVEMBER

No shade, no shine, no butterflies, no bees
No fruits, no flowers, no leaves, no birds – November
– *Thomas Hood*

Monday 1 November

I walked out of the shop this morning, never to return. It was an emotional moment. I have spent years of my life looking after that place and this morning, even before I left, strangers had moved in with hammers and mallets, chisels and saws, to convert my little world into what they thought a bookshop should look like. Most of the work went on upstairs where Mrs Pringle's flat would not look like a flat much longer. I hung around waiting for Blondie the brilliant agent. The buyers had my shop, but had I got their money? He arrived soon after ten to announce triumphantly that £700,000, less his firm's derisory £35,000 five per cent commission plus VAT, had been transferred to my account. Strangely the arrival of more money than I had ever seen didn't quite dislodge my feeling of loss at the sudden disappearance of Mark Hutton Books.

Disposing of the books themselves had been easier than I expected. I got in touch with a man who owns a large bookshop on the south coast. We were thrown together five years ago during a dispute with a maverick publisher who had been trying to shred our profit margin, and there had been a few phone calls since during which we sympathetically reassured each other that selling books wasn't necessarily proof of insanity. He has a sizeable warehouse and agreed to take all my books which he'll pay for on a fifty-fifty basis as he sells them.

I walked down the street, ostensibly a free man. But as I looked at my neighbours – the travel shop, the newsagent, the chemist and the video store – I actually felt cut off, as if I had been dropped from the cast of life's rich pageant.

'I thought you'd walk in here with a smile a mile wide,' Marisa said when I got home.

'I'm unemployed,' I said. 'I'm redundant.'

'You've just got to adjust to leisure, darling,' she said.

We got off on the right foot tonight with a marvellous meal: thin slices of fillets of beef, Chinese pancakes, stir-fried vegetables and crispy seaweed.

'I'm adjusting,' I said.

Tuesday 2 November

Thank God Marisa handled the sale of the shop. She has been showing me some of the paperwork today.

It turns out that the £700,000 was made up of £500,000 for the freehold property, £75,000 for the fixtures and fittings, and £125,000 for the goodwill.

The agent's fee reached £41,125 with VAT, and there were solicitors involved who have charged us £10,000 plus £1,750 VAT. When we claim the VAT back we will have £655,000 – but then another little complication looms: a discussion with the Inland Revenue about capital gains tax.

It looks as if I've retired, but Marisa hasn't.

Wednesday 3 November

A life of leisure stretches before me, but how will I fill it? As November was providing us with a rare sunny day I suggested to Marisa that we took a trip to the coast, but she had a hair appointment at noon.

'Why don't you ring Luke?' she said. 'It's a long time since you've seen him.'

She was right. It was more than two months since we last met, at the Thacker memorial service. I was surprised he hadn't phoned me – I was fairly certain that his fiftieth birthday was about now, and it was an occasion he would characteristically make a song and dance about. I rang his home and Shirley answered.

'You haven't heard?' she said. 'My God, I should have rung you.'

The tone of her voice and the words that she used convinced me instantly that Luke was dead.

'What happened?' I asked, preparing myself for bad news.

'He's in hospital, Mark,' she said.

'What's the matter with him?'

'Perhaps you should go to see him,' she replied evasively, and gave me the hospital and ward.

As I drove the thirty miles to find the answer to this mystery I disconsolately registered the medical misfortunes that were apt to afflict people of our age: the heart attack, the stroke, the wandering blood clot and its friend, deep vein thrombosis. Other more lethal concoctions I couldn't bear to consider.

In a long ward that seemed to run on for ever it took me some time to find him. I kept approaching the wrong bed where the recumbent shape turned out not to be Luke. I finally spotted him in the end bed, lying on his back with only part of his face visible above the sheets. A doctor on his rounds had pulled up alongside Luke who smiled up at me but didn't speak.

'What's the matter with him?' I asked the doctor.

The doctor ignored me, thinking perhaps about patient confidentiality.

'Tell him,' groaned Luke.

The doctor shrugged and looked at me. 'Mr Dyson is suffering from testicular distension, penile blisters and something we refer to as an erotic hernia.'

I hadn't heard of any of these exotic ailments but I caught his drift. 'You mean he's shagged himself into casualty,' I said.

'In layman's language, yes,' he replied sniffily.

I looked down at Luke who lay there in considerable discomfort, sated, scrubbed, shattered and sore.

'It's my fiftieth birthday today and I can't stand up,' he moaned.

'Satyriasis,' said the doctor. 'I think infibulation is the answer.'

I knew what satyriasis was, but I had to look up infibulation when I got home. It meant fastening the genitals with a clasp to prevent sexual intercourse. It sounded a drastic remedy to me.

The doctor strolled off up the ward to what he obviously regarded as more deserving cases, and I pulled up a chair to Luke's bed.

'Happy birthday!'

'No, it's not,' he said. 'I've got erectile dysfunction.'

'I'm not surprised,' I said, and thought to cheer him up with a joke. 'A chap took his out at a party and waved it at an elegant lady. "What do you think of that?" he said. She stared at it coolly and replied "It looks like a penis, only smaller".'

Luke didn't laugh. I had chosen the wrong subject for humour, socially, sexually and anatomically.

'What does Shirley say?' I asked.

'She's disappointed. We were arranging the wedding for next month. She'll be divorced on 10 December, but I'm not getting married in a wheelchair.'

'I should hope not,' I said. 'But you'll be bouncing around by then, won't you?'

'The doctors hope so. At the moment sex is the last thing on my mind, Luckily, Shirley's prepared to wait.'

I didn't know what to say to him. The physical indignities that he was enduring hadn't diminished the yearning for his surgically enhanced partner. He wanted to get fit to suffer more of the same.

'It's just a question of time,' he said.

Memo to self: A man in the grip of an obsession is a tragic figure, particularly if he's got erectile dysfunction.

Thursday 4 November

'I suppose Shirley should feel flattered,' said Marisa when we discussed my visit to the hospital.

Life has already assumed a pleasantly relaxed quality; there are no demands on our time. We take breakfast in the kitchen and share a crossword. Under Marisa's stern guidance my breakfast menu has changed. The frying pan has disappeared with harsh warnings about cholesterol, and I now settle down to calcium-reinforced orange juice, poached eggs and grilled bacon. The butter on my toast has changed, too, and no longer has the same creamy taste. It's an olive spread made with a blend of vegetable oils and olive oil and is, Marisa assures me, good for me.

'Shirley flattered?' I said. 'Do you mean my love for you is deficient because I'm not in hospital?'

'Moderation in all things,' she replied. 'I don't think I could handle a husband consumed by lust. What's "see two water containers", four, three and five?'

'What we ought to do is give Luke a copy of Phoebe's book to read in hospital. A few pages of Maggie Radford's behaviour might cool his ardour.'

'Better still, you should introduce him to Mark. He is a psychiatrist, after all. In Hollywood they'd be treating him for sex addiction.'

'That's "see" as in diocese,' I said. 'It's Bath and Wells.'

She scribbled the answer in the crossword.

'What does the hospital say?'

'They seem happy to let him lie there until he recovers. Time the healer.'

'It's his head that wants healing,' said Marisa.

Wednesday 10 November

The jury are out at the Old Bailey. Charles's fate is now in the hands of eight men and four women who have spent three days listening to the story of the vanished million. They were probably hoping for a lurid trial about sexual athletics below stairs at Buckingham Palace, involving energetic aides and compliant butlers, but instead found themselves stuck with a tiresome story from the financial pages. It was every juror's nightmare and they are getting their revenge now by keeping everybody waiting.

Later: The jury have been sent home for the night.

Thursday 11 November

The judge, irritated by the indecision, called the jury in this morning and said that he would accept a majority verdict. They returned within an hour to say that Charles had been found guilty on all charges by eleven votes to one. A lone juror had obviously been holding out for him.

As usual in this situation it wasn't easy to tell whether the judge thought that this was the right verdict. The prosecution case, as reported in the papers, seemed pretty straightforward. After all, Charles clearly had the money. But there was some doubt about whether, because of some complicated contractual arrangement, he was entitled to it. That, at any rate, was the defence.

The judge, perhaps in deference to this, sentenced him to three years in prison, which was two or three years short of what I was expecting. He should be out in less than two years.

This evening I went to see Janet. I expected to find a distracted lady wrestling helplessly with the new blows that life had inflicted, but was instead confronted by a relaxed woman who thought, in the vernacular, that she'd had a result.

'Oh Mark, it's marvellous,' she said, pulling me physically through the door. 'I thought he'd get eight.' She hurried away, once I was safely in, to find some sloe gin which her observant eye had noticed I liked.

'It's certainly less than I feared,' I said. 'What did he say?'

'Oh he's relieved. What will it be? Twenty months? He knows he can get through that.'

I was curious about whether he would have to return the money, but neither the judge nor Janet thought that this was worthy of discussion. I drank the gin and decided to ignore the subject too. I wondered whether Charles would still be a lord when they let him out but thought that this was also a topic best avoided.

'It was kind of you to come round,' she said. 'I expect he'll become a social pariah now.'

'He'll come back,' I said. 'He's a hard nut.'

She went over to the mantelpiece and picked up some tickets. 'These are for the premiere of Emma's film next Tuesday. I want you to use them. Sadly I won't be able to go. I know what the papers would make of it. Jan's big night out while hubby's in the slammer.'

'The slammer?'

'It's slang for prison.'

'I know. I'm surprised that you did.'

'I've been reading up on prisons, and so has Charles. Know your enemy, he always says.'

Tuesday 16 November

I couldn't quite match Marisa's enthusiasm about going to a film premiere. She said that she had always wanted to attend one, but watching today's 'celebrities' wrapped in absurd dresses to book their place in tomorrow's newspapers wasn't my idea of fun: it was bad enough having to look at them in tomorrow's newspapers. Marisa surprised me by displaying an almost childlike excitement at her proximity to these icons. It wasn't so much the stars, it was what they had chosen to wear.

We saw Emma and Rupert going up the red carpet to shake hands with someone of importance, but they didn't know we were there. I looked for them afterwards to congratulate them on the movie but was told that they had already left for Heathrow because of commitments in America.

The film was good though. In a reverse of Phoebe's story, the villain in *The Devil's Spouse* was a man who treated his women badly. The heroine was his wife who fought a lonely battle against his brutality. She was played by a rising Hollywood star who struggled with great success to produce a British accent. Emma was the girlfriend who replaced her towards the end of the film, and tried to deal with the monster she had inherited. I'm presumably biased but I thought she handled the part brilliantly and could see why she had been given a bigger role in Rupert's new production.

Marisa was very impressed. 'It's funny to think that she was busy in your kitchen all those years with such a hidden talent,' she said.

I had to agree. 'I didn't hold her back,' I said, defending myself. 'It's only because she met Rupert at a keep fit club that she got the chance to show what she could do.'

'I wonder how many undiscovered talents there are out there?' she said. 'For instance, I've often thought that I ...'

'Go for it,' I said. 'I'll support you.'

'... could be an MP.'

She meant it, too.

We made our way through the assembled celebrities to find a taxi. Marisa Hutton MP. After the shocks that the female sex had provided for me this year it sounded quite plausible.

Monday 22 November

Here we go again. More agents, more prospective purchasers. Selling the house is worse then selling a shop because there are more rooms to keep spotless for the procession of hawk-eyed hopefuls who will shortly arrive in droves.

Naturally we chose the agent who put the highest price on the house. A straight quarter of a million is the agreed figure. Property prices in this part of the world left reality behind a long time ago. I bought the place for £70,000, but it will probably cost me a quarter of a million to buy the cottage we want. Roses over the door don't come cheap.

DECEMBER

To perceive Christmas through its wrapping
becomes more difficult with every year.
– E.B. White

Thursday 2 December

I'm divorced – but Marisa isn't. Emma, with her clinical efficiency and Internet proficiency, has freed us both, but Paul Ross, who once promised that his divorce would pose no problems, has now discovered that his religious beliefs will not permit it. The news was relayed to us in a short note that arrived by second-class post this morning.

'He's mentally ill,' said Marisa.

'If not actually unhinged,' I said.

'What do we do now?'

'I go and see him. Perhaps a smack in the mouth will clear his head.'

'His handwriting looks very shaky.'

'I expect writing that letter made him nervous.'

I got into the car feeling surprisingly aggressive. What did the Kung Fu teachers tell you? Never hit anyone unless you're prepared to keep hitting. It wasn't only the disruption Paul had caused in my immediate future which had involved an imminent marriage, it was the sick way he had reneged on his promise to me.

By the time I stood outside their front door the urge to deck somebody was almost irresistible, and I counted to ten before I rang the bell. It was persuasion not punches that might produce the result I wanted.

Andrew appeared eventually looking wan. 'I would like to say what a pleasure it is to see you,' he said. 'Unfortunately that's not possible.'

'Skip the humour, Andrew,' I said. 'Where's Paul?'

'Paul is not well,' he revealed in dismal tones.

'I'm sorry to hear that, but I need to talk to him.'

'Is it the divorce?'

I nodded.

'You'd better come in.'

I followed him into the sitting-room which, with cushions all over the floor, screwed-up newspapers, empty but unwashed cups, crisp bags without crisps, and beer cans, now empty, lying on their sides on the carpet, looked in need of a cleaner.

'Paul's in bed,' Andrew said. 'I'll try to persuade him to come down.'

I stood amidst this scene of chaos and neglect and struggled to believe that Marisa had once lived here. The arrival of Andrew had obviously created a transformation. On the side-board I found some Islamic artefacts, a tin of cannabis, acrylic bangles, and a bottle of energy tablets. How Paul had taken to these changes in his home was hard to imagine. A picture on the wall of Martin Luther King suggested that he had at least had some input in the new dispensation.

He came in wearing an old brown dressing-gown over some pink pyjamas and sat down immediately on the sofa. He looked terrible.

'You got my letter?' he said.

'It arrived this morning,' I told him. 'We were very disap-pointed.'

His face was white and thin and he had the wild stare of a demented eremite. 'Divorce is wrong. I realize that now. Whom God hath put together let no man put asunder. I can't do it, Mark.'

'You promised you would.'

He considered this for a while before answering. 'I've had a lot of time to read lately, and I realized that I was breaking my own rules. God's rules.'

'Divorce is wrong but sodomy's fine, is it?' I said. 'You sanctimonious sleazebag.'

'I don't think abuse will help,' said Andrew, who was sitting on a beanbag on the floor. 'Paul is entitled to his beliefs.'

'And Marisa is entitled to her freedom.' I was so angry that I was on the verge of telling him who Mark's father really was.

'Marisa got married,' Paul said. 'Till death us do part.'

'How could she know that the nice bloke she married was going to turn into a fanatical lunatic?' I asked. 'She's earned remission for good behaviour.'

He sat slumped on the sofa looking sadly at the picture of Martin Luther King, but he didn't speak. It dawned on me belatedly that neither sweet reason nor bitter invective was going to pierce the implacable ideas in his head. I needed a third way quickly and with the shop having been replaced by a large cheque I stumbled predictably on money.

I turned to Andrew who, for all his flaws, was presumably amenable to reason. 'I hear you're planning a taxi firm?' I said.

'That *was* the plan,' he said, 'but with my driving disqualification and Paul's health it's vanished into the long grass.'

'So what are you doing for money?'

'We're completely buggered and screwed beyond hope of recovery.'

'The outlook's not good then?'

'You've got the picture. Losers can't be choosers.'

'I've sold the shop,' I told him. 'I have the money to help you if you want it.'

Andrew looked up, interested. 'We need help all right,' he said. 'Neither of us is working now.'

'OK, here's the deal,' I said. 'Paul co-operates on a divorce and I'll lend you five grand.'

Paul seemed to twitch on the sofa. 'Don't do it. He's trying to buy us. His principles may be for sale but mine aren't.'

Andrew looked at me and shrugged helplessly.

'You're voting for poverty?' I said.

'You heard Paul,' he replied.

Paul struggled to his feet. 'I've got to go to bed,' he said. He shuffled out of the room like a very old man.

'What's the matter with him?' I asked when he had gone.

'Can't you see?' Andrew asked incredulously. 'He's dying.'

'Dying?'

'He was in hospital but he asked to come home. They can't do anything more for him.'

'Dying?' I repeated, unable to believe it.

'And not from what you think.'

'What do I think?'

'Aids, I expect.'

'And what is it?'

'A lethal variety of hepatitis. You could have been easier with him.'

'I didn't know, did I?'

But when I left the house a few minutes later I didn't like myself very much.

Friday 3 December

Shocked by my news, Marisa drove down to visit Paul today but he wouldn't see her. Andrew told her that he looked so bad he couldn't face her, but I suspect that he feared another onslaught about the divorce.

Andrew's major concern seemed to be the house which would belong to Marisa if Paul died. Andrew, looking at the double horror of no money and no home, asked if she would let him live there. She has agreed that he can stay rent free for one year.

Tuesday 7 December

Emma and Rupert have got married in Las Vegas, according to this morning's newspaper. They left the set of their new film, *Hounding Husbands,* to marry in a local chapel. The report adds that among the guests was 'the famous feminist writer Phoebe Davenport whose controversial novel they are filming in Pasadena.'

Thursday 9 December

The sexual casualty is vertical again! In fact he's been home for a fortnight though not quite agile enough to reach the phone. But he rang this morning with his big news and sounded almost normal. Shirley's divorce comes through tomorrow and Luke is marrying her in Brighton on Monday.

It was with some trepidation that I absorbed this newsflash, but I attempted to share his enthusiasm. Such a bold venture deserves all the encouragement it can get.

'Tumescence has returned,' he proclaimed proudly. 'That's a medical term for hard-on.'

'What about the erotic hernia?' I asked.

'Well, I'm on crutches at the moment to protect the muscles, but I'll get rid of them by Monday.'

'Why not get married on crutches? It would give the photographs a certain novelty.'

'Certainly not. We'll be off immediately for a Christmas honeymoon in St Lucia. An emerald isle in a sapphire sea, according to the adverts.'

'And you want to project an image of sun-tanned virile masculinity as you stride across the sand in your thong?'

'A woman of Shirley's extraordinary vitality is hardly likely to repose her hopes in a sexual cripple. I've got to get moving, mate.'

'Was there any advice from the doctors?' I asked. 'Like lay off sex?'

'Yes, there was. They said lay off sex. I expect they go home in the evenings and tell the dog not to chase cats.'

'Anything else?'

'One of them asked if I'd like to talk to a psychiatrist.'

'What did you say?'

'"Is she pretty?" They more or less gave up on me after that.'

Memo to self: I don't blame them.

Monday 13 December

I have bought myself a new BMW and on a wintry Monday morning I drove Marisa to Brighton, not knowing quite what to expect. I have reached that awful age when you are more likely to attend a funeral than a wedding. But Luke and Shirley had arranged it all beautifully. It began in a small register office where the formalities were briskly dealt with, and then shifted to a nearby hotel where they had booked a large room.

There can't have been more than thirty guests, and Marisa and I seemed to be the only ones to have been invited by Luke. The rest were here in support of Shirley's renewed quest to find an adequate male: her parents, Mr and Mrs Appleton, who had arrived from a bungalow in Kent and maintained a discreet and perhaps disapproving silence throughout; sundry aunts and uncles, not quite able to believe the speed at which their niece changed husbands; various co-workers in Shirley's part-time activities – the stables, the nursery school, the meals-on-wheels – and half-a-dozen contemporaries from school who were also known to Marisa.

Shirley, now on her third surname, looked triumphant. Replacing the egregious Andrew with Luke had brought a lustre to her cheeks and made her more Monroe-like than ever. One felt that if Luke could stay upright her future would be idyllic.

His movements this morning were not those of a man who was about to climb the Olympic winner's rostrum, but he shuffled bravely between guests ignoring any discomfort he was feeling.

Marisa was drawn into conversations with the schoolfriends from her past, so I decided to enjoy the company of the champagne. I viewed the day's events with mixed feelings and some misgivings, but the champagne assured me that everything was going to be all right.

At some point a photographer appeared and with minimal material still managed to take more than a hundred pictures. He had been hired by Shirley who wanted every detail recorded.

A buffet lunch was laid out on a long table at the side of the room and we had to help ourselves and then take our food to one of the many small tables in the room.

'How are your old schoolfriends doing?' I asked Marisa.

'They found my story more interesting than their own,' she said. 'One of them used to be in love with you.'

I looked across to where the group were sitting but didn't recognize any of them.

When people had finished eating and were now able to give their undivided attention to the drink, Luke rose to his feet with only the mildest flicker of pain to make a speech. He looked at his new wife and became quite emotional. He talked in tremulous tones about a second chance in life, and about how he had worshipped Shirley all those years ago. He still couldn't believe that he had finally managed to marry her. One of the bride's aunts, stirred by this moving testimony, dabbed her eyes with a table napkin.

When he had finished it fell to me to propose a toast to the happy pair. With great self-control I ignored the suggestions brought to mind by the champagne and eschewed humour. (I had a rather good joke about crutches, but Marisa shot me a look which killed it on my lips.) Instead I delivered a serious and sincere message about the happiness we all hoped awaited the newly-weds. We drank a toast to them, and Shirley came up and kissed me.

'That was lovely, Mark,' she said. 'Do you think he's going to be all right?'

'Be gentle with him,' I said. 'He's only a man.'

Of course the shower of telegrams which used to rain on more conventional weddings was missing, but there were some cards from distant friends and relations, including one from a cousin in Gabon. The most interesting message was an e-mail from Australia: 'Congratulations. The best is yet to come. Love from Nicole and Jamie.'

'I notice they haven't got married,' I said to Luke.

'Nicole's not likely to,' he said. 'She's got too much to lose.'

'So have you. Try to remember what the doctors told you.'

'Doctors,' said Luke. 'What do they know?'

'They know how to avoid erotic hernias for a start.'

At three o'clock we discovered that the car that brought Luke and Shirley to Brighton had returned to take them to Heathrow, and we all went out into the cold December afternoon to see them off. I stood on the pavement hoping that Luke's strength would meet the gruelling challenge of a honeymoon with the versatile Shirley Dyson.

Saturday 25 December

Marisa solved the problem of Christmas with her usual inspiration. We're in Dorset again which is the perfect place for the occasion. Mark, Susie and Samuel are here, Joe is in fine form with the family around him, and even Mrs Wynn has softened, having been almost persuaded that Marisa and I will marry soon.

This wonderful old house has been turned into a Santa's grotto, with decorations, twinkling lights and Christmas trees, but these seasonal embellishments haven't prevented me from beating my son at chess (Nimzowitsch defence) much to his surprise, while Samuel drives round recklessly in his new plastic Jeep. Marisa and Susie had established a formidable alliance before I arrived on the scene, and Mrs Wynn seems happy to follow their wishes on the various domestic questions that such gatherings raise.

So we sat around a roaring fire, drinking mulled wine, discussing the past and entertaining Samuel. Marisa and I had decided as I drove down in my new car that there should be no mention of Paul whose news would cast a pall over the party, and luckily none of them brought up his name.

The Christmas lunch lasted from two until five but at the end it was Samuel and not an adult who fell asleep. He had been up at six exploring his sack and had an exhausting morning playing with his new toys. What impressed me was the way that the television was ignored. This was not a family that required help in passing the time. After a game of Scrabble, an hour was filled with a few hands of poker. Joe won. Then Mark had the idea that we should all play Consequences, a favourite game from my childhood.

The evening passed in a state of blissful alcoholic amnesia, which I thought was how Christmas should be, but I remember one surprising interruption. Mrs Wynn, suddenly vocal, proposed a toast to Marisa and me as 'the future bride and groom.'

I think she was trying to commit us to an event which she still wasn't quite certain would take place.

Tuesday 28 December

Paul Ross died yesterday. Andrew phoned Marisa with the news this morning and I found her in tears. Even expecting the news I was quite shocked myself. We sat in the kitchen and talked about him for an hour.

Marisa recalled happier days when Mark was a boy and Paul a devoted father. I remembered some funny stories from school. *De mortuis nil nisi bonum,*

At least he has been spared the discovery that he wasn't Mark's father, and released from the financial agony that his life had become.

'I'm a widow,' said Marisa, looking sad.

'But soon to be a wife,' I reminded her.

Thursday 30 December

We have found our cottage. We leapt into action this morning after receiving an offer for this house. It was the usual ten thousand short, but my financial adviser, who was making a cake in the kitchen, said, 'Take it. We don't want to spend the next three months arguing about the price. We want to be in our cottage for the spring.'

And so this afternoon, armed with the deceptive prose of the estate agents, we went to view three cottages that Marisa had selected from the fifteen that had been optimistically posted to us. An hour later, with my navigator calling the shots, I drove out of a village and down a narrow lane and there it was, Appletree Cottage, an oasis of tranquillity in the busy south-east.

Marisa's eyes of translucent blue lit up the moment we stepped inside. It had all the things that she was looking for: an inglenook stone fireplace, exposed beams and a flagstone hearth. French doors opened on to a small conservatory, and beyond that was a large, secluded garden (with an apple tree) where I could keep my chickens. The kitchen, in flight from this rustic past, had recently been modernized, as had the two double bedrooms upstairs which each had *en suite* bathrooms.

'It's perfect,' said Marisa.

'But has it got roses over the door?' I asked. 'I forgot to look.'

'It has.'

It is five miles from the sea, and a short walk down country lanes amidst the cow-parsley brings you to the village green where they play cricket on Sundays.

I thought it was perfect too.

Friday 31 December

We offered the full price for the cottage and it's ours. (It was cheaper than we had expected when we began the search, apparently because it has only two bedrooms.) A few frantic weeks lie ahead. We're getting married in London next month and will have moved into our new home before the end of February. I shall then have a home to furnish, a large garden to look after, and chickens to rear. Somewhere in the programme we are going to fit a big holiday. Perhaps we'll go to Australia and look up Jamie Croft.

The startling fact is that it is New Year's Eve and for the first time I haven't bought a diary. My new year resolution is to put all this urgent scribbling behind me. Thousands of words cover dozens of years from the distant memories of a hostile classroom to the sad destinies of Arnold Thacker, Charles Westacott and Paul Ross.

Enough. A new wife, a new home, and a new life deserve a new man. No more maundering, introspective analyses of the daily trivia. Real life is about to take over and this new man, plunged into an unfamiliar outdoor world of birds, animals and flowers, is determined to embrace it.